"You are my wife…." Pietro's shadowed eyes met hers head-on, no trace of doubt or hesitation in his confident stare, though the heavy lids did droop down, hiding their expression behind long, thick lashes.

"Soon to be ex," Marina reminded him, not allowing herself to be intimidated by his merciless scrutiny.

Oh, he hadn't liked that. It was obvious from the sudden flare of something dangerous in the depths of his eyes. But he was no longer dealing with the amazed and overwhelmed girl he had married, the one who had been too naive to see him for what he really was. She'd done a lot of growing up in the past couple of years.

"You are my wife," he repeated. "And as such you will be given what is due to you."

Well, that was a double-edged comment if ever there was one. But which way was she supposed to take it? Marina wondered. As a promise of fair play or a threat of retribution?

"But first there are a couple of conditions."

KATE WALKER was born in Nottinghamshire, England, and grew up in a home where books were vitally important. Even before she could write she was making up stories. She can't remember a time when she wasn't scribbling away at something.

But everyone told her that she would never make a living as a writer, so instead she became a librarian. It was at the University College of Wales, Aberystwyth, that she met her husband, who was also studying there. They married and eventually moved to Lincolnshire, where she worked as a children's librarian until her son was born.

After three years of being a full-time housewife and mother she was ready for a new challenge, so she turned to her old love of writing. The first two novels she sent off to Harlequin Books were rejected, but the third attempt was successful. She can still remember the moment that a letter of acceptance arrived instead of the rejection slip she had been dreading. But the moment she really realized that she was a published writer was when copies of her first book, *The Chalk Line*, arrived just in time to be one of her best Christmas presents ever.

Kate is often asked if she's a romantic person, because she writes romances. Her answer is that if being romantic means caring about other people enough to make that extra special effort for them, then, yes, she is.

Kate loves to hear from her fans. You can contact her through her website at www.kate-walker.com or email kate@kate-walker.com.

THE
PROUD WIFE

KATE WALKER

~ ITALIAN TEMPTATION! ~

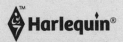

TORONTO NEW YORK LONDON
AMSTERDAM PARIS SYDNEY HAMBURG
STOCKHOLM ATHENS TOKYO MILAN MADRID
PRAGUE WARSAW BUDAPEST AUCKLAND

Recycling programs for this product may not exist in your area.

ISBN-13: 978-0-373-52810-3

THE PROUD WIFE

First North American Publication 2011

THE
PROUD WIFE

CHAPTER ONE

THE letter lay exactly where he had left it last night, right in the centre of his desk. The single sheet of paper was aligned carefully square in the centre of the piece of polished oak, straight in front of his chair where it could not possibly be missed. All it needed was his signature and it would be folded neatly, placed in the already-addressed envelope and sent on its way.

After that there would be no turning back.

But until he made the final move, added the swift, determined scrawl of his signature—the work of just a couple of seconds—nothing at all would happen. It would just lie there, untouched, until he was ready.

Of course it would, Pietro told himself, his mouth twisting wryly at the corners. He hadn't spent almost half his lifetime building up the sort of retinue of employees that any man would envy not to have things that way: staff who would not only obey his every command but anticipate it perfectly, knowing exactly what he wanted and when. They would remain poised, waiting, until he gave the word to act. Then—and only then—would they carry out his instructions to the peak of perfection. It was something he had come to expect so much that he no longer even noticed it, only coming up against the system that created it when something went wrong—which happened so rarely that he couldn't actually recall the last time it had ever ruffled the controlled surface of his world.

He would never allow it to happen: lack of control, wildness of emotion, brought confusion and chaos with it. Confusion and chaos of the sort that he never, ever wanted to experience again.

'Dannazione!'

The curse was torn from him, the flat of his hand slamming down on the polished surface of his desk so that the letter lifted slightly in the air current it created, fluttered, shifted and landed back down again an inch or two to the left before lying still again.

He had known the sort of chaos that could be created by lack of control. Once, just once, he had been fool enough to let that sort of wildness invade his life and take with it the organisation and rule of rational thought he valued so deeply. He had loosened his grip on the reins and lost control. And he had hated the results.

Just once had been enough.

Just once—never again—and it had all been because of this woman.

His dark, brooding look fixed on the letter-heading once again and his fingers clenched, itching to grab the sheet of paper and crush it in his grip, giving in to the heavy pounding of dark anger through the blood in his veins.

Dear Ms Emerson…

That wasn't her true name, of course, but he'd be damned if he'd let his secretary put 'Dear Principessa D'Inzeo', or worse, 'Dear Marina'. Never mind the fact that she was entitled to both names, or that they would stick in his throat if he tried to say them. He hated the thought that his family name was attached to a woman who had given up on their marriage after less than a year and walked out without so much as a backward glance.

Just the thought of her name triggered a rush of images of the voluptuous, red-headed spitfire he'd met when her car had dealt his a glancing blow on an icy London street. The impact of her curvaceous body, green, slightly slanting cat-like eyes and that glorious mane of hair had been immediate. He'd lingered over exchanging insurance details until she had agreed to have a drink with him to finalise things. The drink had turned into dinner and she had never moved out of his life again.

Until after they were married.

Their short-lived marriage had been a total, wretched failure, an ugly spot on his conscience for too long. The searing heat of their hunger for each other had had to burn itself out, but he had never expected it to crash and burn quite so badly—or that the new life he had thought he was going to welcome into the world would in fact be the death of everything he had imagined would be in his future.

It was also appallingly messy, some unfinished business that needed sorting out with everything signed, sealed and made official. Which was the point of the letter.

Pietro paused, raking both hands through his black hair as his blue eyes stared down at the neatly typed letter on the desk surface so intently that the words blurred, becoming totally indistinct. This was what he wanted: freedom from the woman who had turned his life upside down but had never loved him. The chance to slam the door closed on a bitter part of his past, to turn his back on it and walk firmly away, heading out into the future. So what the hell was he doing hesitating, considering…even debating? Why didn't he just sign and send the letter on its way?

He didn't even give himself time to consider the thought. He wanted this over. Done. Finished with, once and for all.

Reaching out, he snatched up the silver pen that had

been lying beside the paper ready for this moment and clicked it open with a firm, decisive movement. This ended now; he was taking his freedom back.

It was the work of just a few seconds to scrawl his signature at the bottom of the page, underlining it with a fierce, hard slash that almost ripped through the page.

It was done—and not before time.

Then in an abrupt change of mood he picked up the letter and folded it carefully, matching the corners with cool precision before sliding it into the envelope that his PA had prepared. The ordinary post wouldn't do.

'Maria!' He lifted his voice so that it carried into the other room, the clear tones strong with conviction. 'Arrange to have this couriered to the address on the envelope, please. I want to make sure it gets there as quickly as possible.'

He wanted to make sure it was put right into Marina's hands so that there was no mistake. He would know that she had received it and that he could finally start to move forward with his life.

His soon-to-be ex-wife would have the freedom to get on with hers too—something he was sure that she wanted every bit as much as he did.

The letter lay exactly where she had left it last night, right in the centre of the kitchen table. The single sheet of paper was aligned carefully square, in the centre of the scarred and worn pine, straight in front of her chair where it could not possibly be missed.

Marina knew that she should read it again, read and absorb it this time. Not skim through the neatly typed paragraphs in a shaken rush, unable to take in exactly what it actually said, only getting a rough and very shocked impression of just what Pietro had written.

When the courier had brought the letter to her door

last night, she had been so stunned to see her estranged husband's name on any communication that she had found it impossible to actually focus on the letter. The words had danced before her eyes, blurring into one dark shadow as she struggled to take in their meaning. And it had been little better when she had gone back to try to re-read it later in the day. She had absorbed just what Pietro was demanding, but she hadn't been able to work out how she felt about it. She had told herself that she would sleep on it and hope that the morning would bring clearer thoughts and guidance on a decision.

'Sleep? Hah!'

Marina mocked her own thoughts as she reached for the kettle and filled it ready to make a much-needed cup of coffee. Sleep was the last thing she had managed; she had tossed and turned, trying to erase or at least ignore the images and memories that had flooded her mind, keeping her from the much-needed oblivion. But, just as during the time when she had been married to him, ignoring Pietro had proved impossible to do. And in the scenes that had played over and over in her head the contents of the letter seemed to grow with every repetition, getting worse and worse until she had finally tumbled into a restless, nightmare-ridden doze.

As a result she needed a large mug of coffee before she could even bring herself to read Pietro's communication over again. She was nerving herself to reach for the letter when the telephone rang unexpectedly, making her start, so that some of the coffee slopped over the edge of the mug and splattered the elegant notepaper.

'Hi, it's me.'

'Who?'

Her eyes were still fixed on the letter, as were her

thoughts, so it took her a moment or two to register just whose voice was in her ear.

'It's Stuart.'

Indignation rang in his tone, and she was not surprised. She had met Stuart in the local library where he was Reference Librarian and he had made it plain that he was attracted to her. His voice should have been easily recognised but, with images of Pietro uppermost in her thoughts, she had been expecting another, very different, masculine response.

The contrast between her estranged husband's sexy accent and Stuart's flat Yorkshire tones couldn't have been more pronounced but she still had to think twice before the truth registered.

'Sorry, Stuart. I'm not fully awake yet. What was it you wanted?'

'I was thinking that we could do something at the weekend?'

'That would be…'

Another glance at the letter caught her up sharp. Stuart might be just what she needed: he was handsome, he was kind, he was nice… But she couldn't accept any dates; she had no right to even show any interest in another man while she was still legally married to Pietro.

'Oh, sorry—no. I—have to go away for a while.'

'Anywhere nice?'

'No—not really,' Marina hedged.

How did you say, 'actually I'm going to see my estranged husband'? She and Stuart might just be starting out on the road towards a potential relationship but she hadn't yet managed to explain to him that Pietro was still in the picture—if only in the distant, soon-to-be ex picture.

Somehow she managed to ease herself away from Stuart's questioning, giving only the vaguest possible answers, her mind only half on the task. The rest of her focus was on the letter that she hadn't yet had a chance to take in.

At last Stuart put down the phone, though not without making it clear that he was annoyed. *Thanks, Pietro,* Marina silently addressed her absent husband. *Not a trace of you in my life for almost two years, and now you make contact again immediately things start to go wrong.*

Or was she exaggerating everything? Perhaps she had misread the letter.

But no; a second, more careful scrutiny of the typescript told her that, not only had she not been exaggerating, but every restless moment of her disturbed night had been fully justified—and then some.

Not only was Pietro suddenly back in her life after having completely ignored her and refused all contact for nearly two years, but he was also back taking control in the way that only he could. She had been summoned; there was no other word for it. Summoned to Palermo. At Pietro's command.

Her husband had snapped his fingers and she was expected to jump. Once more her eyes dropped to the typed words:

> We have been separated for almost two years. This situation has gone on quite long enough. It is time it was resolved.

'You'd better believe it,' Marina muttered. It was more than time that their separation was resolved.

Deep down she had known this was coming, that it was inevitable after her flight from her marriage, the way she had tried to conceal her real reasons for running, the misery of knowing that her husband had never loved her.

Really, she was surprised that it hadn't come sooner. But still she had held out a vain hope. A hope that this letter now dashed to pieces:

…imperative you come to Sicily to discuss the terms of our divorce.

It was so like the first letter he had sent her just after she had returned home following her flight from the misery of their marriage—only then he had been ordering her to come home to take her place once more as his wife. To forget whatever childish nonsense had sent her running in the first place and continue with their marriage as if nothing had happened.

Two years ago and it could still hurt—hurt so badly that just for a moment she doubled up with the pain of it, folding her arms tightly around herself to hold in the distress that almost spilled out of her. She had thought that she had everything she had ever wanted: marriage to a husband she adored, a baby on the way. Then in a terrible twist of fate it had all been taken away. She had lost the baby, her husband and eventually had been unable to stay in the loveless desolation her marriage had become. And now he expected that all he had to do was whistle and she would come obediently to heel like a well-trained dog and do whatever he wanted.

Oh no, Principe D'Inzeo. Not this time! Two long, hard-fought years away from him had given her a strength she hadn't possessed when she had been Pietro's wife.

Rebellion seared through her and she scrabbled in her handbag, looking for her mobile phone. She had no way of knowing whether the number she had was still the right one for Pietro, but quite frankly she didn't care. Simply keying in the text as quickly as she could with swift, stabbing movements of her thumb was some sort of therapy, even if he would never realise the fury with which she'd formed the words.

Why Sicily? You want to talk, you come here.

There!
A final push of the button sent her message winging its way to him and she smiled her satisfaction at the phone as she tossed it down on the table and reached for her coffee once more.

She barely had time to take a sip before the beeping sound announced a response. It was short and to the point— just a single word.

No.

Damn the man. Marina reached for the phone again.

Why not?

Another beep. Another single word:

Busy.

Gritting her teeth, she pressed more buttons.

And I'm not?

Silence.
The screen of her phone remained blank and there was no further sound from it. Marina stared at it, pressed a button and frowned at the empty space that lit up. Surely

Pietro hadn't given up? It just wasn't possible. Pietro never gave up.

Beep. Another message; longer this time.

He hadn't given up. Of course he hadn't.

Jet is ready.

So he was actually prepared to send his private jet to get her there. That was something she hadn't expected.

Car for airport will pick you up in 1 hour.
No.

She could be as ruthlessly monosyllabic as he was—at least by text.

58 minutes…
No way.

This time the reply came back almost before she'd managed the second word. And when her phone beeped again a brief time later she knew what she would see. She was right:

57.
I said no!

She knew she was losing the battle but that didn't stop her fighting. She wasn't just some puppet ready to dance to Pietro's tune while he had total control of the strings. The phone flashed back:

Do you want a divorce?

Did she? Right now it was the thing she most wanted in all the world. Just five brief minutes of letting Pietro

D'Inzeo back into her life, and she wanted out of things as fast as possible. She'd needed the reminder of just how autocratic, how domineering, he could be. The way he wanted everything just the way he liked it and to hell with anyone else's needs.

You bet!
Then get here. 55 minutes and counting...

What was she arguing for? He was right, after all. It was time that the whole sorry mess that had been her marriage was sorted out. Ended. Done and dusted—and filled away under 'Big Mistakes'.

55 minutes, she sent back and could almost sense his reaction of surprise in Sicily or wherever he was as he received the positive response. It shut him up for a while anyway, long enough for her to get upstairs and pull a weekend case out from under the bed.

But as she grabbed her wash bag and dropped it into the open case her phone beeped again and the message she saw on it made her frown apprehensively.

Bring your lawyer, it declared ominously.

He had to be joking. Men like Pietro D'Inzeo might have their legal team at their beck and call, ready to head off anywhere at a moment's notice. But ordinary human beings like her...

All the same, the single taut sentence sent a shiver down her spine just to read it. The note of command was right there in those three words so that she could almost hear Pietro's beautifully accented voice flinging them right in her face.

The thought that he was warning her she would need legal representation made the blood run cold in her veins.

Pietro was obviously anticipating a battle over the

divorce. Probably he thought that she would fight him for every penny she could get. Well, he was going to be disappointed there. All she wanted was for her foolish, youthful marriage to be over and declared null and void. Then she would be able to get on with her own life in peace. She didn't even want any of Pietro's millions, though he was obviously convinced that she would aim for half his huge fortune because she had never signed any pre-nuptial agreement before they had wed.

Well, then, she was looking forward to seeing his face when he realised the truth. Even if that was the only thing she was anticipating with any sort of pleasure about the coming meeting.

But if it was the only way of getting free, which it seemed to be, then she was going to go ahead with it, no matter what it cost her. And, if the arrogant string of commands that had issued from Pietro's phone was anything to go by, her freedom couldn't come soon enough.

With a faint smile she picked up the phone again and pressed 'reply'.

50 minutes, she keyed in, punched 'send' and then switched it off completely.

Let him talk to himself after that, she thought sharply, forcing her mind onto practical matters. She had plenty to do if she was going to get ready and she had had more than enough of Pietro for one day. Even very small doses of him were more than she could take.

So, while she hated having to jump when he called and head for Sicily—hated the thought of coming face to face with the man she had loved so much and who had broken her heart into pieces—it meant that at last she would be free of him.

New year, new start, she told herself. *Think of it that way.*

And, judging by the gloom and swirling snow that was now outside her bedroom window, she would at least be escaping some of the worst of the winter weather. She needed to hold on to the positives when the thought of having to face Pietro again hung over her head like the dark, threatening clouds in the sky.

Just another couple of days and it would all be behind her.

A new year and a new start: at least, that was what she was hoping for.

But first she had to go through the ordeal of seeing her estranged husband once again. Just the thought of that was enough to send a shiver down her spine that had nothing to do with the cold winds and gloomy skies outside.

CHAPTER TWO

PIETRO stood by the windows of his lawyer's office and stared out at the driving rain that was lashing against the glass. His shoulders were hunched, hands pushed deep into the trouser pockets of a sleek silk suit that was the same steely grey as the water-laden clouds above. Impatience made him tap one highly polished black leather shoe against the floor, over and over again.

She was late. They had been waiting far too long. The meeting had been arranged for ten-thirty and it was now almost a quarter to eleven. She was almost fifteen minutes late—if she was even coming, that was.

Expressing his exasperation in a sigh, he raked one hand through the smooth darkness of his hair, narrowing his eyes against the downpour beyond the window. She was in Sicily, at least. Frederico, his driver, had delivered her to the hotel yesterday after picking her up from the airport. He had given her the package of documents that Matteo Rinaldi, his legal advisor, had drawn up for this meeting so that she could have her lawyer go through them and be prepared.

He had told her the precise time of the meeting, so there was no excuse for her lateness. Where the…?

His thoughts came to an abrupt halt in the same moment that down below in the street a taxi pulled up opposite the lawyer's office, stopping in a splash of puddles and a spray of rain. The woman in the back was just a blur through the rain-dashed windows, only the glorious burn of her auburn hair giving any sign that it was indeed his ex-wife.

But that glow of red, hazy though it was, was enough to give him a sharp kick in his guts with the reminder of how it had once looked spread out on his pillows as she lay beneath him, her soft body melded to his. Heat flooded his veins and had him gritting his teeth against the impact of the memory.

'She's here at last,' he said to Matteo, meaning to turn away from the window and step back into the room. But as he spoke the back door of the taxi opened and the woman stepped out on to the pavement.

'She's here,' he said again on a very different note. As he spoke, the woman—Marina—suddenly looked up as if she had caught the words from across the street, staring straight at him; their focused gazes locked and held.

Even from this distance he could see how her vivid green gaze widened and fixed on him. There was no mistaking the way her back stiffened, her head coming up, her chin lifting. There was defiance in every voluptuous inch of her and she held a document case against her body like some powerful shield used to deflect the power of any opposing force.

It was the first time in two years that he had seen her and it hit him with a sense of shock that she was so much the same, totally unchanged—yet somehow totally different, alien and distant from him. And not just because of the barrier of the glass between them.

Another second passed, two, the space of a single heavy heartbeat; their eyes held. It seemed that his breath had died, freezing in his lungs so that he was completely still, not even blinking once. But then another car roared past, spraying puddles everywhere. Marina stepped back hastily and the spell was broken.

A moment later she was hurrying across the road, head down, long legs covering the space quickly, feet in neat black-patent shoes dancing between the puddles. He expected that she would put up the document case to protect her hair but instead she still held it close to her side. But then Marina had always loved the rain.

A sudden vivid image flashed into his head—that of Marina dancing in the rain, her wild hair hanging loose over her shoulders, spinning round her face as she turned. She had been so alive, so full of fun. So beautiful. She had laughed in his face when he had told her to come indoors because she was getting a soaking.

'It's warm rain compared to the stuff in England,' she had declared. 'And I'm not going to melt because of a few drops of water!'

When he had ventured out into the downpour to bring her back inside, she had caught hold of his hands and held him there, forcing him to dance with her too until they had both been soaked to the skin. Only then had she let him sweep her off her feet and up into his arms. He had carried her into the *palazzo* and up to their bedroom, where he had taken his revenge for his drenching in the most satisfying and sensual way possible.

'Dannazione!' Pietro muttered under his breath, cursing himself and his memories as he took a grip on his thoughts and got them back under his control. With a rough movement, he turned away from the window, focusing his attention back into the room and onto the battle that was to come.

Now was not the time for sentimental memories, for recalling flashes of time when he had deluded himself that he was happy. When he had thought that the white-hot burn of passion he felt for Marina was actually love and not something far more basic, far more unmanageable.

Passion had tumbled him into bed with Marina without thought, and the result of that passion had pushed him into a premature proposal of marriage in order to keep her there. To have and to hold. He hadn't been able to bear the thought of her being with any other man, and had seen her unexpected pregnancy as an excuse for putting a ring on her finger to ensure she stayed with him.

Then he hadn't been able to anticipate that there might be a day when he would decide that it was time to let her go. That he would see they no longer had a future together and that the fragile foundations on which their marriage had been built had crumbled to pieces under their feet. He would have laughed in the face of anyone who had told him that such a day would come. Yet now here he was, just waiting for her to sign the papers so that they could draw a line under the mess they had made of things.

The sound of the lift coming to a halt, its metal doors sliding open, alerted him to the fact that she was here. Any moment now his estranged wife was going to walk through that door and…

'Marina…!'

With a struggle he caught back the exclamation, the way that her name almost escaped him. Even though he'd prepared himself for it, the moment she actually appeared in the room still managed to take his breath away. It was as if some force of nature, a blaze of sunlight or a wild whirling wind, had come in through the doorway, freshening and changing the atmosphere in the office.

She looked sensational. The metallic-toned trenchcoat she wore was belted tightly at her waist, emphasising the slenderness there in contrast to the curves of her hips, the full breasts that pushed against the dampened fabric.

Whatever she had on underneath had some sort of V-neck so that nothing hid the fine lines of her throat, the shadowy valley that drew his gaze inexorably downwards until he wrenched it away with a cruel effort. Her glorious hair was darkened by the rain; strands of it tugged free from the confining ponytail in which she wore it. And the weather—or perhaps the dash across the road—had whipped up the colour in her normally delicate, porcelain skin so that her cheeks glowed with colour. Above the slanting cheekbones, her green eyes were strangely dark, the colour of moss rather than the vivid emerald he remembered.

The look she turned on him was blank and distant, totally closed off, as if she had never seen him in her life before. He knew that look; it was the one she had used so often in the last days of their marriage before she had walked out. When he had seen her, that is. Which hadn't been often.

'Signora D'Inzeo…'

Matteo, ever the smooth professional, was moving forward, hand outstretched to greet her.

'Good morning.'

Her smile was brief, controlled, flashing on and off in a second. But it was more than she afforded her husband. The swift there-and-away-again flick of her eyes, the barest lifting of those long, lush eyelashes, granted him minimal acknowledgement as she curled her mouth around his name.

'Pietro.'

It was as if the word had a sour, unpleasant taste on her tongue.

'Marina.'

His own greeting echoed hers, with added ice, if that were possible. He inclined his head the slightest amount possible, then clamped ruthless control over every facial muscle, until even he felt the invisible barriers they had erected between them, the force field of distance and distrust which separated them.

'May I take your coat?'

Matteo was really trying to improve the atmosphere, or at least warm it up by a few vital degrees. But then he was a specialised divorce lawyer who handled cases like this all the time; he must be used to the mood of barely sheathed tension between his conflicted clients.

'Thank you.'

Did she know just how sensual that movement was? Pietro wondered—the tiny shrug that eased the garment from her, thrusting the rich softness of her breasts forward as she put her shoulders back to loosen the fit around them. She probably did, damn her, he admitted, his teeth clenching together in an unconscious response that tightened the muscles in his jaw against the need to make any response. So many times in the past he had performed just that small service for her, had felt the soft skin of her neck and shoulders under the back of his fingers, the silky slide of her hair over his hands as he'd freed her from the garment...

She would turn to smile at him, rub her cheek against his hands, perhaps twist her head to press a kiss on his fingers...

Hell and damnation, no!

Fiercely Pietro dragged his primitive thoughts under control and made himself take a step forward, if only to break the spell that Marina seemed to have cast over him from the moment she'd walked into the room.

'Can I get you something to drink?' Matteo was saying. 'A coffee, perhaps?'

'Some water will be fine, thanks.'

The removal of the coat revealed a crisp, white V-necked

blouse and narrow black skirt: very understated, very controlled, very businesslike.

Very unlike Marina.

Obviously she had chosen the clothes deliberately to convey just the right sort of image. And what image was that? That she was cool and organised and totally in control? In that case, even less like Marina.

The understated look suited her, though. It was undeniably sexy in a very different way. The white top provided a sharp contrast with the rich tones of her hair and the mossy-green glow of her eyes. The slim-fitting skirt flattered her curvy hips and thighs, its shorter length revealing the long lines of her slim legs.

Those hips—and the rest of her body—had more of a curve to them than he remembered from the last time he had seen her, Pietro realised with a sense of shock. In contrast to the glowing woman she was now, then she had looked pale and thin—too thin. Life apart from him obviously suited her, he acknowledged. The thought stabbed him.

The only things about her that were the Marina he remembered were the long, sparkling earrings that dangled close to her neck, gold and multicoloured crystals of different sizes and shapes. They were clearly costume jewellery and a long way from the emerald and diamond creations he had once given her.

'Shall we all sit down?' Pietro asked as his lawyer opened and poured sparkling water into a glass. It was time he took charge.

Once more those green eyes flicked in his direction and, although he had his hand on the back of a chair ready to pull it out, Marina deliberately chose one on the opposite side of the big mahogany table, sinking into it in a graceful movement. She placed the document case on the polished surface in front of her, lining it up carefully and folding her hands on top of the brown leather. Seen like this, she had an almost nun-like composure and restraint. Again, so totally unlike the real Marina that it almost made him laugh. He caught back his amusement with effort. Marina, restrained and composed? The words just didn't go together at all.

He found he rather liked this new image she had assumed. It made him think of the contrast between the outward impression she gave and the person he knew was hidden beneath the conformist clothing. Made him imagine the challenge of getting her out of the subdued garments and freeing the real woman inside. That thought blazed an image into his mind that had him suddenly pulling out his own chair and dropping into it swiftly, so that the barrier of the polished table-top hid the betraying force of his heated response.

As he took his own seat on the other side of the table, Marina accepted the glass that Matteo passed to her and sipped from it carefully. She was still wearing her wedding ring, Pietro noticed, seeing the glint of gold on the fingers wrapped around the glass. It was the last thing he had expected, and he was surprised by the force of his reaction to seeing his ring. It was the ring he had put on her finger after making their wedding vows, still there on the hand of the woman who hadn't even pretended to play the role of his wife for over two years.

'Pietro…'

The sound of his name on his estranged wife's lips jolted him back to the present. He had heard her use his name so many times, but this was like no other time before. This time the single word was both a question and a reproach for the fact that she had said something and, lost in a dangerous blend of angry and erotic thoughts, he had not heard her.

'*Cara?*' he responded, deliberately lacing the endearment with cynicism and knowing he had hit home when he saw her reaction.

Her spine stiffened, her jaw tightened and the soft rose-tinted mouth clamped into a thin, rigid line. Green eyes flashed an uncontrolled response. Now she was letting the real Marina show, he thought with a sense of grim satisfaction. Just for a moment the controlled mask had slipped and she had let him have a glimpse of the woman underneath. This was the Marina he knew of old.

'What exactly are you doing here?' she asked now, her tone making it clear that she wished he was a million miles away.

He dealt her a smile across the table and felt a flare of dark satisfaction when he saw her eyes widen even more.

'We arranged to meet to discuss the terms of the divorce,' he reminded her, calm and reasonable.

Marina took another sip of water and put down her glass with the sort of careful precision that he knew only came when she was really trying to keep a grip on her volatile nature. She wasn't as much in control as she wanted to appear. That made him want to watch her more closely, to see what he could read in her face, in her eyes.

'No, you summoned—*ordered*—me to Sicily so that I could meet with your lawyer to discuss the terms of the divorce. I did not agree to speak to you.'

Oh, he recognised this mood. It was the one where she took everything he said, chewed it up and flung it back at him turned inside out so that it meant the opposite of what he had actually said. It was a mood he knew well. Strangely, it was also a mood that he had missed when she had left him—and *before* she had left him, his memory warned him, giving a nasty, uncomfortable little poke. Just how long was it since he had seen this Marina in his life at all?

'We arranged that our lawyers would discuss the terms, yes,' he pointed out smoothly. 'We will leave everything to them, if that is how your prefer it. But for that we need your legal representative to be here. Where is your solicitor? He is coming later? Soon?'

'He's not coming at all.'

The spark in her eyes, the touch of colour in those alabaster cheeks, the way her head was tilted slightly to one side, her neat chin lifted defiantly, told him he could make what he liked of that.

'For your information, Pietro, not everyone has a lawyer at their beck and call—a man so ridiculously overpaid that he is obliged to jump and come running whenever you snap your fingers.'

From under her lashes those green eyes went towards Matteo just once, briefly, and then came back to fix on his face again. She didn't need to use words to tell him exactly what she thought.

'You gave me precisely one hour to pack and come to Sicily. I had no choice. But I can just imagine what my lawyer would have said if I had even tried to suggest that he do the same.'

Let him make what he wanted of that, Marina told herself. He didn't like it, that much was plain from the way his whole body stilled and tightened in his seat, his head coming up so that his blue eyes blazed into hers. They were like shards of ice, so cold and clear. And she almost felt that the laser-like burn from them might actually mark her cheek where it rested.

When he sat opposite her like this with his back to the windows, he was little more than a dark silhouette, black against the gloomy sky outside. The surprisingly pale eyes in his carved face were all she could really make out—not that it mattered. The truth was that every stunning feature, from the broad, high forehead down to the surprisingly full and sensual mouth, was seared into her memory, impossible to erase. And, if she let them, those memories would destroy her hard-won composure, take her back to the time when she had worshipped the ground this man walked on. To the time that had almost totally broken her.

Just in the moment that she had looked up across the narrow road, and had seen him standing at the rain-dashed window, it had been like the first time she had met him. Then she had seen him through rain-spattered glass too, through the windscreen of her elderly Mini in the middle of an ice storm in a London street. She had been so stunned by the shocking sensuality of the tall, dark stranger's beauty that she had lost control of the wheel just for a second—and had been horrified by the appalling crunch and screeching sound as her car had scraped against the side of his luxurious vehicle.

The world had seemed to spin round her, her breath stilling in her lungs, and she had hardly been able to remember who she was or think to give him her insurance details. In the end she hadn't needed them because he had assured her that the damage was slight and that he would cover the cost of repairs to both cars if she would promise to have dinner with him that night.

She had been totally off-balance where this man was concerned ever since. Just being with him was like being in the eye of some wild, tropical storm every day. She had been swept off her feet, out of reality and into a world of such total delight, wealth and glamour that it had seemed impossible such a fantasy could actually exist.

She had been right about that, of course. She'd had a few short months of perfect delight, total joy—but in the end the fantasy had crashed in flames, burning up all her dreams and illusions as it flared out of control. The passion they had once shared had turned in on itself and destroyed them. Or, rather, it had destroyed Marina, driving her away in misery and pain while Pietro had simply picked up his life and gone on with it as before. He hadn't even troubled to contact her, never mind come after her when she had fled the marriage that had turned into a nightmare. He had sent that one cold command that she return, and when she had refused he had turned his back on her as if she had never existed.

Until now. Until that cold, brutal summons to come to Sicily to discuss the ending of the marriage that had never really been.

When she had walked into the room and seen him standing to one side of the room, dark and inscrutable, watching every move she made, it was as if the past years had evaporated in a second. Every memory, every sensation she had ever experienced, had returned in the space of a heartbeat. All the defences, the armour she had built around herself in order to be able to get on with her life, had disintegrated, crumbling at her feet, leaving her shaken and defenceless when she most needed to be strong.

She had told herself that she would be completely in control for this meeting. That she would be cool, calm and collected when she and Pietro came face to face again. She had done all her crying for the loss of her marriage, the destruction of her illusions in the past, and now she was going to put them all behind her. She had thought that she was prepared because, no matter what she had just said, she had known full well that she would have to come face to face with her estranged husband at some point during her return to Sicily. Pietro wouldn't have ordered her back to the island if he hadn't intended that to happen. He would have to oversee her final dismissal from his life in person, if only to make sure that he was rid of her once and for all. There would have been no point in the summons otherwise. So she had slapped her emotional armour into place, knowing that it made her look hard and distant as a result.

Deep inside, hard and distant was the very last thing she was feeling.

'You don't have a lawyer? You didn't think that you would need someone to protect your interests?'

'And will I?'

Marina made her words a deliberate challenge. She knew her own private reasons why she hadn't felt the need to bring along any legal support, but suddenly she wasn't prepared to reveal those right away.

'You are my wife.' Pietro's shadowed eyes met hers head-on, no trace of doubt or hesitation in his confident stare, though the heavy lids did droop down, hiding their expression behind the long, thick lashes.

'Soon to be ex,' Marina reminded him, not allowing herself to be intimidated by his merciless scrutiny.

Oh, he hadn't liked that; it was obvious from the sudden flare of something dangerous in the depths of his eyes. But he was no longer dealing with the amazed and overwhelmed girl he had married, the one who had been too naive to see him for what he really was. She'd done a lot of growing up in the past couple of years.

'You are my wife,' he repeated. 'And as such you will be given what is due to you.'

Well, that was a double-edged comment, if ever there was one. But which way was she supposed to take it? Marina wondered. As a promise of fair play or a threat of retribution?

'But first there are a couple of conditions.'

'Of course.'

She should have expected that. She *had* expected it. From the moment the letter had arrived summoning her here to this office—Pietro's lawyer's office, on this island, Pietro's home territory—she had known that he intended to show that he had the upper hand. And that he very definitely intended to use it. The sting she felt at the thought of that cold-blooded, ruthless determination turned on her made her flinch inwardly, cursing herself for still being weak enough to let him get under her guard at all. She knew what Pietro was like, didn't she? She should do. She'd spent almost six months as his wife, had seen every side to his character. She knew how cold, hard, how totally pitiless he could be when he was crossed. The lines etched into his face, the burn of ice in those strangely pale eyes, told her that nothing had softened him in the time they had been apart. And the clipped, controlled tone of his voice warned her that he intended to make no compromises, would give no quarter.

'Of course?' Pietro questioned sharply.

'I expected conditions, yes,' Marina returned. 'I'd be a fool not to. You aren't going to just roll over and give in, are you? That's hardly your way. Hardly the behaviour of Il Principe Pietro D'Inzeo.'

'And yet you still came here without a lawyer?'

Just the tone of voice in which the question was asked made her stomach lurch uncomfortably, nerves tying themselves into knots deep inside. It didn't matter that she told herself there was nothing he could do to harm her; somehow there was a tiny little seed of doubt that left her unable to convince her uncomfortable, jittery mind that it was actually true. She might have a secret card up her sleeve, but suddenly she was plagued by a nervous sense of apprehension at the thought of actually playing it.

Pietro D'Inzeo was a powerful man: a Sicilian prince.

Head of the D'Inzeo Bank and all the other companies he'd bought since taking charge of the D'Inzeo business empire. A man with huge riches and influence. She knew from having seen him in action that he never suffered fools gladly, that he was a cold-blooded predator in the business world and that, when crossed, he made a very dangerous enemy. And she was planning to thwart whatever plans he had made for the way this meeting was to go. She was—hopefully—going to checkmate him here in front of his lawyer. A proud Sicilian like Pietro wouldn't take that lying down.

But, even as the question slid into her thoughts, she instinctively pushed it right out again. If there was one thing she was sure of, it was that Pietro's sense of honour, his proud Sicilian character, would always ensure he played fair. It had never been the thought of the financial implications of this meeting that had worried her.

The emotional repercussions were a very different matter.

'I didn't think I'd need one. After all, there are laws about this sort of thing.'

Seeing the way Pietro's dark brows snapped together on hearing that, her nerves twisted once more deep in the pit of her stomach. For one desperate moment her heart ached with the memory of the way that hard, carved face used to change when he'd been with her. How those icy eyes had softened, the beautiful mouth curved into a smile. How she had once been able to kiss away that frown between his brows.

'And besides,' she added hastily, 'you said I'd get what was due to me.'

'I did say that,' Pietro acceded, his tone not helping things very much.

'So perhaps you should let me know about these conditions.'

'Of course.'

It was Matteo, Pietro's lawyer, who spoke. After a swift glance at his employer's stony face, earning himself a brief nod of agreement, he now came to sit down opposite Marina, opening a file of papers he had placed on the table between them.

'It is time we got down to business.'

Marina tried to turn her attention to the lawyer and what he was saying, but it was difficult when the stinging awareness of Pietro and everything he did, every movement he made, was rushing through her like a charge of burning electricity. She was conscious of the way he seemed to have backed down, conceding the central role to his lawyer, but she knew that any such concession was deceptive, totally misleading. He poured himself a drink of water and curled long, tanned fingers around the glass but never lifted it to his lips. He even leaned back in his chair, apparently at his ease—but out of the corner of her eye she could sense the tension that held his long body stiff, watchful and alert.

He was observing everything that was happening, watching her so closely that she almost felt her skin singe under the heat of his gaze. She knew that, although Matteo was speaking, it was Pietro who was in control, his lawyer only the mouthpiece for what he wanted to say.

'The conditions...?' she prompted hoarsely, wincing at the way her voice cracked on the words. Struggling for control, she focused every last bit of her attention on the older man opposite her, trying to blot out the fact that Pietro was even there.

'I don't think that you will find them too difficult,' Matteo assured her, tapping the sheaf of documents with an elegant silver pen. It was the same file that had been delivered to her on the plane, the one she hadn't even opened, never mind read. Because the one thing she had ever wanted from this man was his love and, when she'd realised he had none to give her, there was nothing else that could fill its place.

'Firstly,' Matteo said, drawing her attention away from that thought, 'you must agree to give up the name D'Inzeo and revert to your maiden name.'

'Willingly.'

The condition had been one she was expecting so she felt a rush of relief that this was all it was.

She meant it, she tried to tell herself. She really did. Bitter memories of the past put a depth of feeling into her response that must surely convince Pietro, even if she couldn't convince herself. Once she had been so very happy to have Pietro's name as her own. It was a name with a long-lived Sicilian history, the name of centuries of princes and princesses, hugely wealthy bankers who had a much more prestigious place in the world than her own ordinary middle-class family. She had been proud to have it as her surname, amazed at the deference and response that it brought with it, the speedy effect just mentioning it would create—an effect that Pietro treated with casual disdain.

But most important to her had been that it was the name of the man she adored. And it should have been the name of her baby too. The cruel slash of pain that thought brought with it pushed her into unguarded speech.

'Why would I want to keep the name of the man whose marriage to me meant nothing to him?'

To his lawyer's right, she heard Pietro snatch in a sharp, angry-sounding breath from between clenched teeth. Her throat tightened, knotting itself against the lurching beat of her heart as she tensed, waiting for his furious response.

But it never came. The look that Matteo flashed towards Pietro silenced whatever outburst had been about to escape his ruthless control and he subsided into silence again, merely indicating with a swift, impatient flick of his free hand that the lawyer should continue.

But Marina couldn't be unaware of the way that the other hand, the one still wrapped around his water glass, tightened against the hard surface until his knuckles showed white, revealing the fierce struggle he was having with himself to hold back the angry words that had almost escaped him.

'I will have no trouble with that particular condition,' she managed stiffly, still keeping her eyes on Matteo's calm, controlled face.

'Buon.'

The silver pen made a small check-mark against the relevant paragraph in the document.

'Next, you will sign a confidentiality agreement, promising never to speak of your marriage, never to reveal anything of your life with Principe D'Inzeo, either during the time you were together or of the reasons why you split up.'

'I… *What?'*

Now she had to turn to Pietro; she couldn't stop herself. She knew that her eyes were wide with anger and disbelief—and, yes, a savage degree of pain—when she turned them on the man who sat silent and immobile as a rock.

'You want me to sign…?' she managed, but then the hurt got the better of her.

How could he think that she would ever want the world to know the truth about their life together? That would mean letting everyone know about the way she had been so bitterly disillusioned. The baby…

From nowhere came the thought that, if their baby had been born, it might have had the same pale, devastating eyes as its father and suddenly it felt as if the sides of the room were closing in on her, taking all the daylight with them, making it difficult to breathe.

'How dare you?'

If she had thrown the words at the wall opposite, it could hardly have responded less. Pietro's reaction was to narrow his eyes until they barely gleamed from behind the darkness of his lashes as he sat back in his chair, watching and waiting.

'I have my name to protect.'

'But you can't really think that I would do anything to damage it?'

When Pietro blinked slowly and eased his position in the chair, he looked like nothing so much as an indolent lion, lazily considering the question of whether it was worth the trouble of pouncing. There was enough controlled menace in his stare to make her reach for her water glass and snatch at a quick gulp of the drink so as to ease the uncomfortable dryness of her throat.

'And can you say the same for your boyfriend?'

'What boyfriend?'

She didn't give Pietro the chance to answer that, rushing on instead in her determination to refute his implied accusations.

'Just who do you think I am? I have had nearly two years apart from you. Two years! And in all that time did I so much as give an interview or get my picture in a magazine?'

'You didn't have your freedom then,' he drawled coolly. 'And you had a comfortable allowance that meant you needed to keep me sweet.'

'No, I didn't. Do you ever check your bank statements?'

Marina challenged when one black eyebrow lifted in a cynical questioning of her assertion. 'Or do you find it hard to notice when a paltry million is missing—or not—from the many hundreds of millions you have coming in and out each month?'

That had him finally sitting up straight. The flash of anger in the glare he turned on his lawyer was so sizzling that for a second Marina almost expected to see the elegant Matteo shrivel into a pile of smoking ash right where he sat.

'I said…' Pietro began, but a strong sense of fair play had Marina rushing to the other man's defence.

'Oh, I know—I can imagine what you said, or rather *ordered*, would be done. And I'm sure that poor Matteo did just as you commanded. But you can't order me around. I'm not married to you now.'

Pietro's beautifully sensual lips twitched into a wry smile that mocked her passionate outburst.

'Are you implying that I was ever able to order you around?' he enquired sardonically. 'Because believe me, *bella mia*, that was never the case. In truth, I doubt that anyone has ever been able to order you to do anything. So are you claiming that you never used the allowance?'

'No—I'm not *claiming*!' Marina pushed back the annoying strand of hair that had worked loose from her ponytail with an impatient movement. 'I'm *telling* you: I never used the allowance you sent. Not a penny.'

'Why not? That money was for your keep.'

'Why not? I would have thought that was obvious. I don't need to be kept. I have a job—I went back to the library. I earn my own living. I don't want anything from you. I never did and, now that we're not married, I never will.'

'Might I remind you that we are at present only sepa-rated?' There was an odd edge to Pietro's voice, one that roughened it shockingly at the edges. 'We are not yet divorced.'

'Not yet,' Marina admitted. 'But it can't come soon enough for me. I just want it over and done with—signed and sealed so that I can get out of here with my freedom and never look back.'

'In that case,' Pietro returned imperturbably, 'perhaps you will let "poor Matteo"—' he echoed her words mockingly '—get on with things.'

But Marina had had enough.

'No, I don't think so. I don't think we will "get on with things".'

She pushed back her chair, thought about getting to her feet and then hesitated. A few moments more and it would have had much more effect. She was actually quite enjoying seeing Pietro off-balance for once. He didn't quite know how to take her—and for now that was exactly how Marina wanted it.

'What things, Pietro?'

She directed the question straight into his watchful face, seeing the faint scowl that drew his dark brows together, frowning over narrowed eyes.

'What things—more terms? More conditions? More dictates from the great lord and master, Il Principe D'Inzeo?'

'Marina…' Pietro's use of her name was low-toned, deep, a strong note of reproof on the single word.

'More "thou shalt do this" and "thou shalt not do that"? "Thou shalt not speak to the press"? Do you really think I'd want to let the scandal mags know the truth about our marriage?'

She was letting her tongue run away with her but somehow she couldn't even bring herself to care. This was why she had come here, why she'd felt she had to put herself through the ordeal of seeing Pietro one last time. She had wanted to try to voice—partly, at least—the things she had never been able to say when they had been married. To try to provoke him into reacting, into something other than the carefully measured, icy distance that was all that he had showed her in the end. All that the once heady, burning passion had burned down into, cold and ashy.

'Do you think I'd want the whole nasty, miserable mess spread out in the tabloids—our dirty washing hung out to dry in full view of the public?'

'Marina…'

It was definitely dangerous now, definitely a warning. His eyes were blazing cold fury, and the hand that had held the water glass now drummed a warning tattoo on the polished table-top. But it was a warning Marina was well past heeding. She had the bit between her teeth, and she wasn't going to be called to order by anyone.

'You think you can toss me some instructions and if I want your money I'll do as I'm told, will follow your conditions to the letter?'

'I think you'd better listen to what those conditions are.'

'No.'

Marina shook her head firmly, sending her auburn ponytail flying with the deliberate emphasis she put on the movement.

'I don't need to hear them.'

She heard Pietro's breath hiss in sharply, watched his sharp, white teeth snap together and the muscles in his jaw tighten ominously.

'Marina—you came here so that we could discuss the terms of our divorce in a civilised manner.'

'No.'

'No?'

That really shocked him and the flood of triumph she felt as a result had a devastatingly intoxicating result, rushing through every nerve and vein like the powerful effect of some richly potent brandy.

'No—that's not what I came here for. In fact these "discussions" are nothing to me. Because, you see...'

Now was the time for her to get to her feet, and she pushed back her chair so that it almost overbalanced with the force of her action. Now was the time for her to stand upright so that Pietro had to look up to her as she straightened her shoulders, lifted her chin and looked straight down her nose at him.

'I only have to follow your instructions, agree to your *conditions*, if I want anything from you. That was the bargaining card you thought you held—the one that gave you some sort of power over me. But you were wrong.'

Stooping to pick up the document case she had brought in with her, she turned it in her hands until it was just in exactly the right position. Her defiant green eyes met his coldly assessing blue ones with as much determination and strength as she could muster.

'You only hold those bargaining cards if I take anything at all from you—that's what you counted on, and that was where you went wrong. Because you see, Your High and Mightiness, Principe Pietro Raymundo Marcello D'Inzeo, I want nothing at all from you—nothing.'

She had to pause for breath there, and when she did she expected that he would break in on her, that he had to say something. But still Pietro sat immobile, still as a sphinx. He barely even seemed to be breathing, he was so motionless, so ruthlessly in control. Only his eyes burned with something so fierce, so dangerous, that just for a moment Marina's heart lurched, her nerves stuttering. Then she pulled herself together, drew a deep, unsteady breath and rushed on.

'I came here today not to discuss terms but to give you them.'

Zipping open the leather case, she pulled out a sheaf of papers that exactly matched the ones in front of both Pietro and Matteo, the ones from which the lawyer had been reading the list of conditions.

'I've seen your offer of a divorce settlement and I've decided to reject it—totally and completely.'

At last Pietro moved, even if it was only his mouth that opened to speak in a voice that was deadly and low.

'Then you'll get …'

'Then I'll get exactly what I want, husband dear— exactly what I came here to tell you I'll take from you— and the answer is nothing. Absolutely nothing. Because I came into this marriage with nothing and I'm going out of it with exactly the same. So you can take your divorce settlement and put it—put it wherever you like. Because I want none of it!'

As she finished speaking, she tossed the documents down onto the table in front of Pietro where they landed with a heavy thud, the impact throwing up the loosened pages and sending them flying up into the air—straight into her husband's icily controlled and rigid face.

CHAPTER THREE

'I WANT none of it!'

The sound of Marina's voice died away, to be replaced by the fluttering of the papers still settling down on the desk in front of him. Then the room was filled with silence, a silence so taut and intense that you could have cut it with a knife.

At Pietro's side, Matteo had dropped his pen from his grasp and seemed to have frozen into statue form. The young secretary who had been sitting at the far end of the table, keeping tactfully quiet and trying to look inconspicuous as she took notes, was staring, goggle-eyed, with her mouth wide open.

All this Pietro took in with a single swift glance before turning his attention back to Marina. To his wife. The wife he had thought would soon be his ex.

All she had had to do was to accept the terms of the divorce he had offered and sign on the dotted line.

Instead of which…

She was still not fully back under control after her outburst of just moments before. Her chest was heaving as if she had run a marathon, the generous curves of her breasts lifting and falling with each irregular, snatched gasp of air. And the effect of her loss of temper, together with the effort of getting her breathing under control, had sent a rush of colour into those normally pale cheeks, so that now they were delightfully flushed with pink in a way that no clever make-up, no matter how subtly used, could ever achieve.

Above that wash of rose, the green eyes were bright with emotion, sparkling wildly under the thick, black lashes. Her hair had escaped from its fastening and was now starting to tumble down around her shoulders in casual disarray.

This was the woman he had first met. The woman who had knocked him off-balance so that he couldn't think straight. She looked wild. She looked defiant. She looked magnificent. If truth be told, she had never looked so damn good—not even on their wedding day, when she had been as stunningly beautiful as he had ever imagined it was possible for a woman to be.

Perhaps later, on their wedding night—lying in their bed with that glorious hair spread out around her, bright against the creamy colour of the pillows; her mouth swollen with kisses and her green eyes deep and dark with the pleasure that came from sexual satiation?

No!

Furiously Pietro clamped down on the erotic thoughts that threatened to escape his control and forced himself to focus back on the situation in hand. He'd let them take charge once before, and look where that had got him.

The silence had stretched out now almost to breaking point, neither the secretary, nor indeed Matteo, daring to make a move to break it. Marina's still slightly ragged breathing was the only sound in the room other than the sudden lash of rain against the windows as the rainstorm outside started up again.

It was as Marina's wide green eyes met his, clashing sharply, that Pietro launched into action. Pushing back his chair, he got to his feet, one hand shooting out in a commanding gesture.

'Everyone—out!'

His pointing finger indicated the door, but there was no need. Already Matteo and the secretary were heading in that direction.

So too was Marina. She had swung round on her heel and was marching out.

'Not you!'

In a swift, pouncing movement, Pietro was round the table and at her side in a couple of determined strides. Reaching out, he caught hold of her arm, his fingers clamping tightly around her wrist when she would have ignored him and moved on.

'I said, not you.'

The look she turned on him was mutinous, defiant, and he felt the muscles under his grasp tighten in instinctive rejection. But to his surprise she didn't put up the struggle he anticipated, the resistance she clearly wanted to use. Perhaps it was the fact that they were in his lawyer's office. Perhaps she realised that she couldn't just fling that challenge—and the papers—right in his face and walk out. She must have known he would only come after her. That they would have this out sooner or later. 'Sooner' seemed to suit her.

And sooner definitely suited him.

'Just what is going on?' he flung at her as soon as the door had closed behind the other two. 'What the hell are you playing at?'

Marina's face was a mask of pure rebellion and her eyes flashed rejection of his closeness, his words. But she answered him at least.

'I'm not *playing* at anything. I meant every word I said.'

'But you can't. I mean, why the hell would you?'

'Why the hell would I *what*, Pietro?' she flung back at him. 'Turn down your offer of a divorce settlement? Reject the money you would be prepared to give me if I would only accept your small, petty conditions?'

Of course, by 'petty' she didn't mean small and insignificant; Pietro felt his jaw tighten against the furious response that almost escaped him.

'I was offering you a generous—'

'I'm sure you were,' Marina cut in sharply. 'After all, you are a very wealthy man and, as I said, there are laws about these things.'

This time he couldn't hold back on his anger, outraged by the fact that she would consider that was all that mattered.

'You think I was only offering you a settlement because of what the law says?'

Just for a moment their eyes locked together, clashing sharply so that he saw the moment her expression changed, saw the defiance and provocation leach from her gaze, leaving it darker and more subdued   a mossy green flecked with gold, rather than the sparkling, flashing emerald of just moments before.

'No,' she conceded, glancing down and away as her sharp white teeth worried at the soft flesh of her bottom lip. 'No, of course I don't think that.'

'Then why...?'

His question brought her head up sharply. The look in those wide eyes twisted something deep in his gut that had him fighting against responding, against showing the burning rush of reaction that seared through him.

Hell, no! Frustration, anger, shock and disbelief were already a volatile and treacherous mixture, one that had him disturbingly off-balance when he wanted to be fully and tightly in control. Add in sexual desire to that potent blend, and it was even more dangerous. All it needed was a single spark and the resulting explosion would take his head off.

Sex was what had brought him and Marina together. Sex was what had kept them together, even when things were falling apart. Sex was the one thing that had never died between them, at least for him. And sex, damn it to hell, was what was still there.

With the width of the table between him and Marina, it had been bad enough. She had still been able to get to him—physically, at least—just as she always had. But he had been able to tamp it down, put a lid on it, keep it under control.

But now, with her eyes burning into his and her curvaceous body up close, it was so much harder to impose restraint. The scent of her skin was in his nostrils, sweet as a rose, mixed with some faintly herbal tang from the shampoo in her hair. He could feel the warm softness of her flesh and the delicacy of bone under his fingers, the contact sending electrical pulses of heat along every inch of nerve. It was all he could do not to give in to the demands of his senses.

'Why?' Marina echoed now, her tone subtly different. 'Why did I turn you down? Isn't it obvious?'

'Not to me.'

Then, when she lifted a russet eyebrow to question his response, and those green-and-gold eyes flashed another challenge straight at him, he gave her the real truth.

'All right, I will admit that I am torn between two possible explanations.'

'Two?' She hadn't expected that. 'What two?'

'One—' Pietro lifted the first finger of his free hand to mark the point '—you think that if you play hard to get with this then I will increase the settlement—give you more to keep you in—what is it you say?—the manner to which you have become accustomed.'

'If you think that, then you couldn't be more wrong!' Marina protested, but Pietro cut across her with his second point, adding another finger to the first.

'Or, two, you really don't want this divorce at all. So you believe that if you pique my interest enough then I will—'

'Don't want this divorce?'

Marina's tone was sharp with disbelief and she was shaking her head swiftly and violently in rejection of what he was saying.

'You can't possibly think I don't want it, that I...that I want to come back to you? Is that what you're saying?'

She couldn't be hearing right, Marina told herself. He couldn't have said any such thing. But even as she let the thought into her mind she suddenly knew a shock of recognition of exactly why he had said it.

In the moment that he had caught hold of her wrist she had tensed against the restraint. She had tried to pull away but he had held her, kept her there—without force, but also without effort—while Matteo and his secretary had left the room. Then they had been alone.

And that had been her opportunity to break free, to ease herself from his restraining grasp, fight with him over it, if need be. Instead she had become so absorbed in the argument between them that she hadn't even thought to insist on her freedom. She had stayed right there, close to him, her wrist in his hand for all the world as if she *wanted* it—as if she wanted to be that close.

And Pietro, being the man he was, had interpreted her behaviour in exactly that way. It was something she had to disabuse him of—and fast.

'And, while we're talking about things I don't want,

would you mind taking your hand off my arm? You're hurting me.'

'My apologies.'

It was cold and stiff, and he let go so fast that her hand dropped to her side. It was only as she felt the cooling rush of air over her skin that she knew a sudden shiver of regret at the loss of his touch. After two years' separation, the warmth of his fingers against her flesh had had a familiarity that seemed shockingly right. One that had her lifting her arm to cradle it close to her, feeling the loss as a wrench at her heart.

'I am sorry,' Pietro said again, less stiffly this time.

'Oh, no, you're fine,' she managed, unable to let him believe he might have hurt her. 'It's nothing.'

She even waved her arm around between them to prove that there was no damage. But her uneasy gesture only created more tension in her already twisting stomach when she saw that those pale eyes didn't follow the rather wild movement, but remained fixed on her face. And there was a new, disturbing darkness about them, one that made her shift uncomfortably, moving her weight from one foot to another and then back again.

He was so close, physically so close, and yet emotionally so very far away.

She might have thought that two years away from him would do much to dilute the impact he had on her. But the truth was the exact opposite: it was as if she had been starved for all of that time so that now, when she was presented with a glorious feast for her eyes and her senses, she didn't know where to look, what to absorb first.

His hair was black, and glossy as polished jet, and even in the darkness of the rain-soaked day it gleamed with health. His olive skin still had the lingering tan of high summer, in stark contract to her own winter pallor, and the burning ice-blue of his eyes blazed above the high, slanting cheekbones in his carved face.

He had never been one to wear much in the way of cologne or aftershave, but with the familiarity of memory she could catch the scent of the lime shampoo he had used when they'd been together and apparently still favoured now. Even more memorable, and agonisingly bitter-sweet with the thoughts it aroused, was the clean, faintly musky scent of his body that came to her as he moved and that lingered on her arm where he had held her.

Unthinkingly, she rubbed at the spot where his fingers had touched her skin, reviving that scent and sending it whirling around her, so that she closed her eyes for a moment against the impact of it.

'I know.'

His tone pulled her from her memories, flung her eyes wide open to stare at him. Something that wasn't quite a smile flickered over Pietro's mouth and his gaze held hers with a shocking intensity.

'I know. I feel it too. It's still there, isn't it?'

'I don't know what you mean.'

Marina took an uneasy step backwards, acknowledging privately that she knew exactly what he meant, but unable to stop herself.

'There is nothing *still there*.'

'Liar,' Pietro inserted smoothly, silkily, and he matched her step away from him with one of his own towards her. Slow, careful, nothing in it to frighten her—on the surface, at least. But the burn of his hooded eyes made her stomach tie itself in knots.

'I'm no liar—I don't know what you're talking about.'

But she did. She knew exactly what he meant. He had only to touch her and her whole body was fizzing with it, sensual heat stinging along every nerve.

Pietro shook his head slowly.

'I'm not afraid to admit that I still want you. I'd be a fool to even try. I don't want it to be there any more than you do, but at least I'm not scared to acknowledge what there is between us. As you should, if you'll only be honest with me.'

'I'm not scared!'

Not scared? Who was she kidding? It had always terrified her, this irrational burn inside her, this primitive intensity of need that took away her sanity, her sense of self. No one else in the world had been able to set it off in her, but it seemed that when Pietro was anywhere near she simply inhaled it on the air they both breathed.

It scared her, but it also thrilled her like nothing else in her life had ever done. And the truth was she missed that thrill.

'If you want honesty then, yes—all right—there's always that. There's always sex. But there has to be more to a relationship than passion.'

'It's a damn good place to start.'

Pietro's smile, the touch of laughter in his eyes, was temptation itself. He could entice the birds out of the trees and right into his hands when he switched on that charm. She had thought that she had come here knowing just how that charm worked, and fully armoured against it. But the truth was that determination was no shield against the effect he had always had on her.

'But we're not starting anything, remember?' Marina reminded him pointedly. 'We're here to *end* our marriage. That was the whole point of this meeting.'

'That was the point at the beginning,' Pietro agreed, but his tone implied something else entirely, sparking off a new wave of uncertainty.

'What do you mean "at the beginning"? You can't be thinking of going back on your decision?'

Pietro's shrug dismissed her question without giving away anything of what he was thinking. His face was a total mask, his hooded eyes opaque and hidden.

'You were the one who changed the terms of agreement,' he said with a sideways, slanted glance towards the table where the bundle of papers she had flung at him still lay in a tumbled mess, tossed every which way. 'You refused the settlement I had on offer.'

'Because I didn't want to take anything from you!'

He nodded slowly, eyes never leaving her face. Another step forward, closer. He wasn't dangerous or threatening. Just *there*. So very much there.

'You changed everything. So now we have to discuss— renegotiate under a very different set of rules.'

This was impossible. If she had been asking for more than he had been prepared to give, she might understand that he would baulk at the thought of agreeing to that. But this…?

She saw her freedom, the hope of a new future, fading away from her—or at the very least receding into the distance instead of coming closer at last.

'That's ridiculous! You can't want me to take things from you? You can't refuse to go ahead with the divorce because I'm asking for *less* than you originally offered.'

Surely Pietro couldn't possibly be petty enough to refuse the divorce just because she had rejected the terms on which he offered it? No; she knew that with absolute certainty. Pietro D'Inzeo was many things—forceful, domineering, arrogant, cold, uncaring—but petty was not one of them. Which meant that something else had made him change his mind, decide they needed to renegotiate. And it was that 'something else' that tugged on nerves that were already stretched taut.

Pietro had moved again, coming closer still. Yet somehow she couldn't make herself take the necessary steps back and away from him. Her mind seemed to split in two: one half told her that she was staying right where she was because she didn't want him to think for a moment that she was as scared as he accused her of being.

The other half simply wanted to stay still, to wait for him to come closer, for no other reason than that she *wanted* him close. Wanted what the darkness of his eyes telegraphed. The sensual promise that had no need to be spoken.

She wanted that. She wanted the taste of him, the feel of him. The warmth of his body surrounding her. She wanted it just once more. And she'd wanted it from the moment she'd walked into the room and seen him standing, dark and dangerous, by the window.

The truth was that she needed that danger. Right here, right now, no matter what the consequences. It was what had been missing from her life for the past two years. And, if this was her only chance to know it one last time, then she wasn't going to turn and run from it. She might have admitted that it scared her but the reality was, now that she was back under the influence of that fizzing, burning excitement, the thought of a future without it frightened her even more.

She still wanted Pietro—physically at least. She always had and probably always would. She might not be able to love this man any more, their marriage might be broken beyond repair, but she wanted him so badly.

So she stayed her ground and waited. She looked Pietro straight in the eye and never blinked or backed down, waiting to see just what he had planned.

And frustratingly that had the exact opposite effect of

what she had anticipated. Pietro came to a halt, just out of reach, a frown drawing his black brows together.

'Are you aware that you are giving off totally mixed messages?' he said slowly, pale eyes searching her face as if trying to probe the answers to the questions that were in his thoughts. 'One moment you are telling me you want nothing from me—that our marriage is at an end. That you feel nothing. The next…'

His dark head went back, that assessing gaze sweeping over her, from her head to her toes, seeming to take a protective layer of skin where it landed.

'And I do—want nothing,' she managed, aiming for confidence and missing it by a mile. She knew it from the way one of those brows lifted, challenging her declaration.

'That's not what your eyes are saying,' Pietro murmured, his voice soft and silky in a way that lifted all the tiny hairs at the back of her neck. 'Or your mouth.'

'My…?' Marina tried to question but her throat was too tight, her lips too dry, so that the words died before she could speak them.

Nervously, she slicked her tongue over parched lips, only realising that she had betrayed herself completely when she saw his beautiful mouth curl up in a hint of a smile.

'So which is it, hmm, *belleza*? What exactly do you want?'

'I…'

Marina couldn't find any words to answer him. Her head felt as if it was filled with cotton wool, clouding and numbing her thoughts. The ground underneath her feet seemed just as flimsy and insubstantial, shifting and yielding like dangerous quicksand, so that she could barely keep her balance. She closed her eyes against the sickening feeling. She knew what she should tell him, what she had resolved to tell him when she had set out on her journey to Sicily.

She had been so proud of her decision to throw the divorce papers in Pietro's face. She'd been so determined to tell *Il Principe* that she wanted nothing from him, that she was walking out on their marriage and leaving everything behind. That feeling had even taken away the sting of being summoned so autocratically by the man who had destroyed their marriage with his cold and callous behaviour, the dread of seeing him again.

That thought had buoyed her up all the way here. It had carried her through the first dreadful meeting, held her spine straight and her head high as she'd struggled with the desperately painful memories that simply seeing him had revived. She had just been waiting for the moment when she could throw her defiance and his settlement right in his face, and then she would be out of here, free as a bird, escaping to her new life. And, if the scars that her marriage had inflicted on her heart hadn't actually fully healed, well, at least she wasn't going to slash them any deeper.

That had been the plan. But, instead of now being out of here and free, somehow things had been turned upside down. Her carefully planned rebellion had fallen as flat as a deflated balloon. Far from seeing it as the final word in her rejection of him, Pietro seemed to have taken it as some sort of encouragement to begin again. To think about reviving the marriage from which she had been trying to escape.

And which she had been totally convinced he couldn't possibly want at all.

'Too late.' Pietro's voice was shockingly close, bringing her eyes open in a rush to find that he had closed the distance between them swiftly and silently and was now standing right beside her.

'I don't…' she began, but he shook his dark head slowly,

blue eyes locking with green holding her gaze effortlessly.

Reaching out a hand, he laid a long finger across her lips to silence her.

'Too late,' he repeated. 'You don't need to say anything. Your silence said it for you.'

'No...' Marina tried and immediately regretted the fact that she'd even opened her mouth. Because just the small movement needed to say the single word had brought her lips, and very briefly her tongue, up against the clean, tanned skin of that strong finger.

And that was just enough to taste him, absorb the slightly salt tang of his flesh. A taste that immediately sparked off such a rush of sensual, intimate images that her head swam as they flooded into her thoughts. Memories of the times that she had kissed him, known the feel, the scent, the flavour of his skin. When the intimate aroma of his body had driven her almost to swoon in pleasure, as she had tried to get nearer, closer, yearning ever closer. Never ever satisfied until their bodies came together, combining the two of them into one.

'No,' Pietro said in a very different tone from the one she had used.

His hand slid under her chin, tilted it so that her face was lifted towards his. There was no escaping the burn of his eyes, the warm brush of his breath against her skin. If she had hoped to hide her reaction to him, she realised it would be impossible. Surely he must see her response in her face, in the catch of her own breath as she looked up at him? And her pulse was thundering so hard inside her head that she felt sure he must hear it too.

'You're still dodging away from putting this into words, so I'll do it for you: I want this. You want this. So let's stop wasting time.'

And, before she could catch her breath to give him any sort of response, he lowered his head and took her mouth with his own.

CHAPTER FOUR

IT WAS no good even trying to deny the way she was feeling, Marina told herself as the firm, warm pressure of Pietro's mouth took control of her lips. She wouldn't be fooling anyone—least of all herself.

This had been inevitable from the moment she had first faced Pietro across the table, and known that the time they had been apart had had no impact on the way she felt about this man physically. She had walked into the room convinced that she had armoured herself against him. But she had been lying to herself.

Telling herself anything had no effect. It did nothing to make her senses stop feeling as if they had come home. It couldn't send back into hiding the needs that one single touch of his mouth had brought out, blinking and stumbling into the bright light of day. Needs that only took one moment of exposure to the heat of awakening to grow wild and uncontrollable, destroying any chance of holding on to her sense of self-preservation in the space of a heartbeat.

She was swaying on her feet, leaning up against him in the need to feel the hard strength of his body against her; the power of muscle and bone kept her upright when she felt as if she was melting in the heat of the response that seared through her. She wanted this man. She had always wanted him from the moment they had met, and the passage of time had done nothing to reduce the yearning sensation his kisses awoke in her. All she had done by keeping away from him was to let the need build, grow stronger and stronger inside her, until all it required was the tiny spark of Pietro's touch, his kiss, to break through the dam she had built around her and flood her senses with aching hunger.

'Pietro…'

His name was a choking cry from her mouth, the hunger too great to allow her time for anything more. Even the few seconds' break away to gather in a needed breath was too long, too much. She snatched in air and then immediately lost it again under the pressure of his wicked mouth, the tormenting slide of his tongue that enticed her lips to open up to him, to let him deepen and intensify the kiss. And, if her heart had been thundering before then, now it felt as if the pressure of her pounding pulse-rate would explode inside her brain, the primitive rhythm of her blood drowning out all other sound, even that of her own thoughts.

Pietro's hands were in her hair, tugging the covered band that bound her ponytail down and away, sending her burnished locks tumbling about her shoulders where long, powerful fingers tangled in the silky fall, twisting tight to hold her prisoner, keeping her head exactly where he wanted it. He angled it so that he could indulge his sensual hunger to the full.

It had been too long since she had felt like this. Too long since she had known this heated, sensual connection, this rush of pleasure through her blood, flooding every nerve. Too long since she had felt this hunger uncoil in the pit of her stomach.

'Too long,' she sighed on another much-needed intake of breath, and found that her words were being echoed by Pietro's voice, thick with passion, roughened by need.

'Far, far too long,' he agreed, hands tightening in her hair, lips coming back to take hers with even more force of passion.

She was being moved, pushed, half-walked, half-carried backwards across the room until her spine hit the wall, Pietro's body crushing her against it. With her head falling back against the hard support, he could find her mouth with even more force, even more passion, and he took full advantage of that fact, plundering her lips with renewed intensity. Marina went with him, yielding one moment by giving him the access he sought, the next kissing him back, tongues tangling together in the dance of passion.

They had forgotten, or were oblivious to, where they were. Awareness of the lawyer's office, the formal boardroom-table and chairs, the rain-lashed windows, faded totally under the force of need that had them in its grip. It was only when a soft, polite tap at the door—one that had to be repeated before it registered, causing them to pause—brought them reluctantly, unsteadily, back to reality.

'*Principe*… Signor D'Inzeo?'

Matteo Rinaldi would only risk interrupting his important client if he really had to, Marina recognised dazedly, her impression reinforced by the way Pietro's head whipped round. He directed a ferocious question in angry Italian at the man on the other side of the door. The following exchange was too fast, too furious for her to catch it, and the truth was that she was incapable of thinking clearly enough for her limited knowledge of their language to be helpful in following it.

Her head was spinning, her thoughts whirling. But it was not just the abrupt interruption of their passion, the shocking ending to Pietro's kisses, the wrenching of his mouth away from hers that had her reeling so hard she could only be grateful that the wall was at her back to give her support. She feared that she might actually fall to the floor.

What *was* she doing? Had she taken total leave of all her senses to let this happen? Not just *let* it but actually indulge it, share in it, *encourage* Pietro's actions with her own heated and mindless response.

Mindless, indeed! And totally, naively stupid.

'Stupid, stupid, stupid!' she berated herself in a furious whisper under cover of the staccato argument in Italian that was still going on over her head.

Hadn't she known what it would be like? Shouldn't she have already guessed that this was how Pietro operated, the way he won people—women—round to his way of thinking?

But she *did* know, and that was the appalling thing. She had first-hand experience of just how his seductive technique could be used to scramble a woman's brain, reduce her to a mindless mass of quivering jelly—a mindless mass of quivering, sexually molten jelly totally at his mercy. Wasn't that the way he had dealt with her own fears that they were rushing into marriage, that they didn't know each other well enough?

He had laughed at her concern and then, when she had persisted in her anxious questioning, he had soothed her with gentle, seductive words and even more gentle, even more seductive, caresses.

He had distracted her thoughts with his touch, taken over her mind with his kisses, reduced her to a mess of wanton need. Then, when he had finally 'given in' to her hungry pleadings, he had taken her to bed as an act of forgiveness for the fact that she had ever doubted him. And he had made love to her with such skill, such passionate intensity, that by the time she had come down off the ceiling again and back to reality she'd no longer even been able to remember what it was that had worried her so much, let alone have enough brain power left to question him any more about it. She hadn't wanted to, anyway. She had loved him, and the truth was that she had wanted to marry him, even if the circumstances of their rush to a wedding hadn't been the very best.

But the fear that he would use those same seductive techniques against her once more had been the reason why, when the later, more devastating fears had assailed her, she had fled the house and her marriage as fast as she could without ever seeing him again. She had been too terrified that he would work his sensual magic on her once more and keep her from facing the reality that there was nothing but sex holding them together once the promise of the baby they had married for had been taken away from them.

And she had almost let him do the same to her all over again. Almost. She had been adrift on a hot, wild sea of burning passion, a hunger so savage that even now her body still throbbed with need. If Pietro's lawyer hadn't had the nerve to knock at the door, bringing his employer's wrath down on his unfortunate head, then she would have...

She didn't dare to think of what she would have done, the way she would have given in to the sexual mastery that Pietro had over her and that she had never ever been able to deny.

'Everything is fine.' She heard Pietro fling the words towards the still-closed door. Whatever had concerned the lawyer, he wasn't prepared to risk aggravating his employer's fury by actually opening the door and coming in.

'Correction,' she inserted, loud enough for Pietro to hear but not for the words to be totally distinct from the other side of the door. 'Everything will be fine—if you'll just get *off* me.'

She accompanied the words with a forceful push at Pietro's broad chest, catching him unaware with his attention directed towards the conversation with his lawyer. She knew a moment's satisfaction at seeing him knocked off-balance, then a quick, sliding movement had her away from his imprisoning frame and out of reach before he could quite collect himself.

'What the…?'

If he hadn't seen it happen with his own eyes, Pietro thought he would have found it impossible to believe the change in Marina in what seemed like no more than the space of a couple of heartbeats.

The ardent, responsive siren he had been kissing had turned into a woman of ice. Her face had frozen into the cold distance of a marble statue. Her beautiful green eyes that had been brilliant as emeralds, then dark and soft as moss, were now pale and opaque, completely shut off from him. A few moments before she had been sexily ruffled, burnished hair tumbling around her pale oval face. The restrained, neat secretary's clothing had been messed and rumpled, the cream top pulled out of the waistband of the slim skirt—his doing, of course. While his mouth had been locked to hers, his hands had been busy getting to know the shape of her all over again, the softly feminine contours of her body. And as a result he was hard, hot and hungry, the yearning to bury himself in her a bruising ache deep down. It was all he could think of, all he wanted.

'What are you playing at?'

He hardly recognised his own voice, it was so raw and husky, sounding as if his throat had been scraped raw. He could barely control the sense of outrage, the feeling of being led on and then dumped hard and fast, as he watched her busy herself with swift repairs to her appearance. She was calmly smoothing down her clothing, tucking it in here, straightening it there. She even combed her tangled hair through with her fingers, twisting it back so that it hung once again in the long, sleek tail halfway down her back.

How could she do that? How could she switch off so completely, locking herself away as if they had never connected in any way at all? It stung him with memories of how she had done that before at the bitter end of their marriage. The way she had retreated from him, turned her back on him, eventually shutting him out altogether. It had seemed that even the passion that brought them together had died.

But that kiss just now had proved otherwise. It was still there, that wild, fierce, primitive fusion between them, one that still burned its way through his body like some stinging electrical current that couldn't be controlled.

'I said...' he began, again and at last she looked up, opaque green eyes locking with his probing stare.

'I know what you said,' she returned, cool and calm as you like. Infuriatingly so. 'You said that before as well. And my answer is the same.'

When he frowned his confusion, she flashed him a defiant look from under those long, long lashes.

'I am not playing at anything. In fact, the truth is that I have never been more serious in my life. I came here to end my marriage and that's what I intend to do.'

'It looks like it.'

That earned him another glare, but this one flashed real fury, total rejection of his comment.

'Oh, are you assuming that one kiss—one lousy kiss—is all it takes to have me begging to come back to you, into your life, your marriage?'

'I thought it was *our* marriage,' Pietro inserted with icy precision and watched her eyebrows shoot sky-high in an exaggerated expression of fake surprise. He felt his jaw tighten against the temptation to rise to her provocation of that 'one lousy kiss'.

'*Our* implies that we were equal,' she flung at him. 'And I would say that equal does nothing at all to describe the marriage we had.'

'You think I forced you into it? Or used some sort of blackmail? You were willing enough at the time, as I recall.'

'Willing, yes. But then I was half out of my mind with—with wanting you. You were the one who insisted on marriage.'

'Because you were pregnant.'

It had been unplanned, a mistake, the result of a stomach upset and a missed pill, but still he'd snatched at it as an excuse to rush her into marriage. Back then, he hadn't been able to bear the thought that she might even consider not coming back to Sicily with him when his time in London was up. Just the idea that she might be with anyone else had driven him half insane with jealousy, so he'd used the fact that she was carrying his child as a reason to ensure she became his.

'Yes—because I was pregnant and you were so insistent on your precious D'Inzeo heir being born legitimate that you didn't give me time to breathe. Or think.'

'You needed to think about it?'

'You bet I did—or I really should have done. If I'd been in my right mind at the time, then I would have recognised that there was nothing between us to build a marriage on.'

'There was a child. I wanted that child. And I wanted you.'

He knew he'd rushed and grabbed at the excuse, but he

had thought that was what she'd wanted too. And he had believed that, like him, she had been happy at the prospect of the baby, that it was wanted even if it hadn't been planned.

'You wanted the baby, all right. And you wanted me because we came as a pair. But if we hadn't been pushed into things because of my pregnancy we would both have seen that what we had—all we had—was a white-hot fling. A wild, sexual affair. The flames were inevitably going to burn out between us, and sooner rather than later. One or both of us was bound to get tired of things.'

'As you did.'

The look she flung him was dark with bitterness, empty of all warmth. Did he really have to ask? those expressive eyes said. Wasn't it so blatantly obvious?

Of course she'd got tired of things—of him. It was what she'd said in the letter she'd finally sent him two weeks after she'd walked out— that she was tired of the whole thing and wanted her freedom back. That she had already been regretting their rush to marriage before the loss of their baby.

When she had lost the baby early into that marriage, he had been devastated at the loss of the future he had thought was ahead of him. Unable to hide that feeling, and concerned that showing it would make Marina feel that he was disappointed in her, he had buried himself in work. Work that had turned out to be his salvation when, with every day that passed, she had withdrawn from him further, eventually shutting him out altogether. He had moved out of their bedroom on the doctor's advice to give her space during her recovery time. She had never shown any sign of wanting him to move back.

He'd tried to talk her round—or rather, he'd kissed her round. Seduced all the fight out of her and transferred all that fire and energy to their bed. In spite of himself, he couldn't hold back a smile at the memory. She hadn't—she couldn't have been faking that.

It had just been a temporary truce in the slow disintegration of their relationship. He'd thought they were on their way to a similar ceasefire a few moments before. She'd melted when he'd kissed her, softening in his arms and kissing him right back. And just for a few seconds it had been as if the break-up had never happened. If only Matteo hadn't decided to come knocking at the damn door…

'You didn't give me time to think then,' Marina persisted. 'But I really don't need time to think now. Or, rather, I've done all the thinking I want to do about this—about you, about our marriage. I want out once and for all, and nothing you can do is going to make me change my mind.'

'Maybe you should wait until you know what's on offer before you start saying you don't want anything.'

'I told you I don't want anything. Nothing that's over there…'

A rather wild, dramatic gesture—by the hand with her wedding ring on—indicated the scattered documents on the table.

'And that goes for your money—and your damn kisses.'

One lousy kiss…

She even wiped the back of her hand across her mouth as if she wanted to erase the feel of his kiss, the taste of his mouth. She must still be able to taste him because he could still sense the traces of her kisses on his own lips. Hell, if he slicked his tongue across his bottom lip it would feel as if she had kissed him all over again.

And she had responded, damn her. She hadn't—she couldn't have—been faking that.

One lousy kiss…

If Matteo hadn't interrupted things, she could have been his by now. Right here, right now on the thick red carpet—or up against that wall if need be. It had been all there between them once again: the fire, the heat, the hunger. She had wanted him and he had craved her so much that he was still aching for her. His body was still in a tumult of need, one that he had barely managed to get under control.

No matter what had happened between them, he still wanted her as much as the day he had first taken her to bed. More so because of the almost two years of separation—twenty long, empty months without her in his bed had been like starving in the desert with no food to eat, no water to slake his thirst.

He still wanted this woman more than any other woman in the world and he was damned if he was going to let her go without having her at least one more time. Without working out this hunger that she awoke in him simply by existing, driving him to distraction. He wanted her to the point of madness and somehow, come hell or high water—and probably hell—he was going to have her again before he let her walk out of his life.

But that meant somehow he had to persuade her to stay and, knowing Marina, that wasn't going to be easy. If he said push, he knew very well that she would pull—right in the opposite direction.

But he was not going to let her get away from him. He'd work with opposites if he had to.

'Fine. You've made your point.'

Marina stared at Pietro in blank confusion as he shrugged his shoulders and turned away from her. Had he really just conceded, even as she was nerving herself and strengthening her spine to face further attacks? It seemed that he had as he turned away, strolled—*strolled!*—to the other side of the room.

'Have you read all of these?'

As he spoke he was picking up the sheaf of papers she had flung at him in a fury of rejection, smoothing, straightening, arranging them in the right order. With the documents in his hands, he turned slightly, looking her straight in the eye.

'No.'

What was this, some sort of test? Was he holding out temptation to her, waiting to see if she wavered, if she hesitated at all? If she thought again about the divorce, or about the settlement she could get from it? A cruel knife seemed to slash across her soul at his apparent conviction that money was what mattered here. That money would be what motivated her, nothing else.

'There was no point in doing that, was there? There's nothing you could offer me to make me want to stay.'

Pietro had collected up all the papers and returned them to the file, tapping it against the edge of the table in order to make everything neat, tidy, perfect. And that brutal knife twisted in the wound it had inflicted on her as he did so. What was the point in having everything neat and tidy, carefully aligned, when it was recording the death of something that had once been so wonderful? Or at least that she had thought had been so special. Her disillusionment had been bitter when she had realised that Pietro had never felt the same.

When he had learned she was pregnant he hadn't hesitated. No D'Inzeo child was going to be born illegitimate, he'd declared and at the time she'd simply been so grateful that he wasn't furious with her for the mistake she'd made, that he wasn't going to walk out on her, that she hadn't cared that his proposal hadn't come with ardent declarations of love and happy ever afters. He wanted to marry her and that was enough. The rest would come in time. Or so she'd told herself. She had enough love for both of them and the baby would bring them even closer together.

She hadn't reckoned on the tragedy that had overtaken her. The way that the wedding flowers had barely had time to fade and wilt before she had woken in the night with terrifying cramps tearing at her body. By the time the next day had dawned, she had lost her baby. Miscarried his precious heir.

'You can destroy them completely as far as I'm concerned. Toss them into Mount Etna or throw them out into the sea. Anything. Get rid of them once and for all.'

If only she could do the same with her memories. Wipe from her mind the very different way that Pietro had reacted to the loss of their child.

Where she had been devastated, shattered, lost in mourning, he had been calm, distant, controlled to the point of coldness. And his attitude had driven home to her the way that she had failed.

She had failed him by being unable to deliver the one thing he had married her for, and nothing had been the same after that. Not even the desire that had once blazed so hotly could bridge the chasm that the loss of their baby had opened up between them.

Unable to bear it any longer, wanting things over and done with, she marched across the room and flung open the door, revealing the lawyer who was still standing there waiting for his client's next command.

'Come in Mr—Signor Rinaldi. I think it's time we really got down to business.'

'And by *business* you mean—ending our marriage?'

Was she hearing things or had there been some sort of a hitch in Pietro's voice as he asked the question? With her back to him she couldn't see his face, but really she knew it wasn't possible. It would be like seeing a tear in the eye of a tiger just before it pounced on some defenceless prey.

'Of course. What else could I possibly mean?'

Slowly he turned to face her, his expression closed off, frozen into the blank mask of some carved marble statue.

'Fine. But if you don't want all this…'

The pale-eyed glance took in the room, the offices, those documents once more, before he tossed the file into the nearest wastepaper bin.

'Then we don't need lawyers or courts to wrap things up. We can handle this on our own. Matteo, consider yourself dismissed from this case.'

'Principe…' the lawyer began in protest, but Pietro held up a hand to silence him.

'My wife and I will talk this over in private, then we will call you back to make the legal arrangements. Is that not right, Marina?'

'I— It—'

Marina didn't know how to answer him. It sounded as if she was finally getting exactly what she wanted. At least, that was how Pietro made it seem. But she hadn't anticipated the 'private' discussions her husband had decided they needed.

'Yes,' was all she could manage, even as her mind was still processing what Pietro had said.

Being 'private' with Pietro was exactly what she had hoped to avoid at all costs. Yet, if she didn't agree to it, what hope did she have of ever leaving Sicily with the divorce and the freedom that she had told herself she wanted so desperately?

Her resolve might have been shaken for a moment when Pietro had taken her in his arms and kissed her, but if anything that had only shown her just how much she needed to do this. She had to get away, out from under his malign influence and into the hope of a new life, before he gained control of her again. Before the dark, erotic spell that he wove around her simply by existing closed over her head again and dragged her down into the sensual mindlessness in which she had existed when she had first met him.

If a short time talking things over was what was needed in order to ensure that happened, then surely she could cope with it? Forewarned was forearmed, and she was already well armoured against Pietro's seductive techniques. That near-miss earlier had reminded her of just how much she needed to be on her guard.

So, 'Yes, if that's what's needed,' she managed.

'*Buono...*'

Pietro's nod was a gesture of dark triumph. He reached for the raincoat she had discarded on a chair on her arrival, shook the creases out of it and held it up, ready for her to put on.

'Where are we going?'

'First I will drive you back to your hotel.'

'There's no need.'

Just meeting his eyes made her want to take a step backwards—more than a step. But that would be to give away what she was feeling and she was determined not to do that.

'There is every need. You will drown if you go out in this.' A flick of his head towards the window indicated the rain that was still lashing down. 'It is hardly the act of a gentleman to allow his wife to go out in a thunderstorm when he can provide transport.'

Did he know how that word 'allow' infuriated her? Very probably he did, and that was exactly why he had used it. There was a challenge in Pietro's brilliant eyes as he spoke.

One that heightened as he saw, and clearly understood, the struggle she was having with herself.

'What are you afraid of, *cara*?' he murmured softly, the question meant for her ears only. But the challenge was there in his tone as well, and in the way that he raised her coat very slightly, holding it ready for her.

'Nothing!'

Pure exasperation drove her forward, and she turned to push her arms into the sleeves of the coat he held out, letting him lift it up and on to her shoulders—which was exactly what he had planned all along, she knew. It left her feeling like some puppet, very much at the mercy of the man who held all the strings in his hand and used them to direct her as he wanted.

'Does this look like fear?'

'Of course not.'

His smile said that he had read her face perfectly, that he knew of every second of her battle with herself and, worse, that it was just what he had aimed at. As he adjusted her coat around her, lifting her hair out from where the collar had trapped it, smoothing it over her shoulders, she had to bite down hard on her tongue to keep from betraying herself and letting him see just how badly he had got to her.

He'd challenged her to do exactly as he wanted, knowing only too well that she would rather die than to show him she was afraid. And now she was trapped into following his lead, at least until they had had that 'private' conversation.

But how difficult could he make it when the only place they were likely to have this conversation was in some public spot—the bar at the hotel, or some other restaurant? She would actually be much safer there than anywhere else. Safe from this man, at least.

Her thoughts and tangled feelings were quite a different matter.

Just his closeness was already affecting her again. The scent of his skin, the soft touch of his hands, the brush of his fingertips over her hair and down over her shoulders as he adjusted the fit of her jacket, all awoke memories she had fought long and hard to bury out of sight. Under her clothes her skin remembered the caress of those bronzed fingers, the trails of fire they had traced all over her body.

Clenching her jaw tightly against the feelings, Marina turned her attention instead to Matteo and his secretary, making a performance out of saying goodbye and thanking them, until she felt that Pietro must surely be fit to burst with impatience as he waited for her.

'I appreciate your help and concern in this,' she said, shaking the lawyer by the hand.

'My pleasure…'

Surely even the lawyer must sense the atmosphere, the swirling undercurrents of tension and distrust that eddied about them, clogging the air with antagonism and suspicion? But infuriatingly, when Marina turned back to where Pietro was waiting by the door, it was to see that he was still leaning against the wall, shoulders relaxed, arms loose, looking as if he had all the time in the world. Once again he had checkmated her, and not until she actually stepped towards the open door did he make a move to straighten up.

'Ready?' he asked, his tone as relaxed as if they were just about to go out on some casual lunch-date or afternoon trip somewhere.

'Ready,' Marina echoed, knowing there was no way she could match that careless manner.

'Ready' was exactly the opposite of the way she felt. And

there was no way that she was ready for whatever Pietro could have in store for her.

He might act calm and easy-going, but she had no doubt that there was so much more, something far darker and more dangerous than the pleasant mask he was letting her see.

Her unexpected move to declare she wanted nothing from this divorce but her freedom had thrown him at first, wrong-footing him in front of witnesses. And experience had taught her that no one caught out Pietro D'Inzeo like that, not with impunity.

He would want to make sure he regained the upper hand as quickly as possible. And Marina knew that that was exactly what he planned.

What she didn't know was what he meant to do once he had it.

CHAPTER FIVE

THE rain had slightly eased by the time they approached the main door of the hotel, the name of which Marina had grudgingly given him. Frowning through the water-lashed windscreen, Pietro found that he didn't know whether irritation or an amused acknowledgement of Marina's fiercely stubborn spirit was uppermost in his mind when he saw where she had stayed the previous night.

It was worse than he remembered, he acknowledged, noting the shabby paintwork and the worn stone steps. It might be in the historical centre of the city, close to the Massimo Theatre, but that was about all it had going for it. Which left him wondering just why she had determined on choosing this particular place when she could have been much more comfortable elsewhere.

She should have been so much more comfortable. He would have footed the bill, and she knew that. Which of course, knowing Marina, he reflected wryly, was precisely why she had done the exact opposite of what he had suggested.

And that brought him back to his suspicions as to just why she was behaving this way. Did she really want absolutely nothing out of their marriage? Or was she just playing a provocative game, aiming for some other sort of prize?

If she truly wanted nothing at all from him, then why hadn't she initiated the divorce herself sooner? Or was it the arrival of this man Stuart in her life that had changed everything? Pietro's frown darkened into a scowl and his hand tightened on the wheel until the knuckles showed white.

'We're here.'

It was the first time that Marina had spoken since they had left Matteo's offices. She had perched herself on her seat, head upright, back stiffly straight, knees pressed tightly together. She had put her black leather handbag on her knee and held it there as if it was some sort of security blanket on to which she was clinging for dear life.

She had stared straight ahead, green eyes focused out beyond the windscreen, the silent barriers of defence closing around her until he felt totally locked out. Well, that was something he was used to. She didn't even need locked doors to close him out.

The creamy purity of her elegant profile with its long, straight nose and high, slanting cheekbones could have been carved from alabaster, it was so distant and unresponsive. Yet somehow that very purity made a disturbingly sensual kick straight below his belt so that he had a hard job concentrating on driving through the busy, narrow streets in the inclement weather conditions.

It was the rush of blood downwards in his body that brought a sudden clarity and a cold, controlled determination to his rational mind. He was damned if he was going to let her dance back into his life and then waltz right out of it again. If there was one thing that kiss in his lawyer's office had taught him, it was that he still wanted her—physically, if not emotionally. And that was the one thing he was going to act on.

He was sure that he could persuade her that it was what

she wanted too. Her response to that kiss had been so open, so revealing, so deliciously sensual, that he knew she felt just as he did, though she would go through all the fires in hell before she would ever admit the truth. But if he let her out of the car and into the hotel then what was to stop her disappearing straight into her room and not coming out again? She might call a taxi round to the back of the building and head for the airport before he could do anything.

His attention was caught by a flurry of movement near the hotel door, a gathering of people far too close to the steps that led into the foyer. He didn't need to see the cameras, the microphones, to know exactly who they were. He had enough experience of being hounded by the paparazzi to recognise them instantly.

Somehow the news had got out that Principe Pietro D'Inzeo's errant wife had come back home, temporarily at least, and already the press pack was scenting blood. The fact that Marina had been staying in such a downmarket hotel would have only whetted their appetites for the potential scandal behind the facts.

'I said, we're here,' she added more sharply when he made no response. 'This is my hotel.' One hand waved in the direction of the dilapidated building.

'I am aware of that.'

Now at last her auburn head turned in his direction, and out of the corner of his eye he caught the look she flashed him in reproach as he didn't make a move to turn the car towards the kerb.

'Then would you please slow down and… You can park just here. *Pietro!*'

The furious emphasis on his name reminded him of just how wildly impulsive and unpredictable his wife could be. He had once had cause to be glad of it because her impulsiveness had rushed her into his arms, into his bed, before either of them had really had time to think. But right now, in this particular situation, he had no wish to risk her taking matters into her own hands and trying to escape. Stretching out a hand, he pressed the control that implemented the central locking, hearing it click smoothly into place in the same moment that Marina's breath hissed in swiftly through her clenched teeth as she realised exactly what he had done.

'Just what the blazes are you playing at?'

'No game,' he assured her. 'Believe me, *carina*, this is no game. I never play where such things are concerned.'

'What sort of things?' she questioned sharply, tugging at the door, trying vainly to open it. 'Let me out of here!'

'No way.'

Pietro shook his dark head, sending a lock of black hair falling loosely over his forehead so that he had to toss it back with a swift, abrupt movement.

'I said that we needed to talk—in private. And that's what we're going to do.'

'We could have been private in the hotel.'

'Oh, sure,' Pietro said scornfully. 'With a couple of dozen scandal-hungry paparazzi waiting at the door ready to rip the flesh off your bones, if it would give them the best possible story for tomorrow morning's papers.'

'The papar...' Marina twisted round, her hair flying as she struggled to look back. 'They were there?'

A curt nod was all the response she got. It would help if he could get down the street more quickly, but the weather and the press of midday traffic meant that he had to crawl at a speed that made him clench his jaw, impatient to be at the end of the road and take the route to the coast.

'I didn't see them.'

'Then it's just as well I did,' he tossed at her. 'Otherwise it would have been like feeding a lamb to the wolves.'

'Oh, come on!' Marina protested. 'They wouldn't have been that interested—what is there for them to want to investigate? Only the fact that...'

The words faded from her tongue when she saw the look he turned in her direction, the blaze of something dangerous in the darkness of his eyes.

'Only the fact that the Principessa D'Inzeo has unexpectedly returned to the island after fleeing from her husband's home after less than a year of marriage.' Dark anger sizzled along the words, mirroring the burn of his gaze. 'And the chance to dig about again in the grubby details of the past and the way that the marriage that had seemed so perfect suddenly crashed and burned so dramatically.'

'Oh...'

'They never did manage to find out what went wrong a couple of years ago.'

Pietro steered the car round a tight corner.

'So now they would enjoy building it up into the worst possible scandal they can manage.'

'But there isn't...'

Marina couldn't finish the sentence. Just the thought of the paparazzi and the reporters digging around in her private life made her throat close up over anything she wanted to say.

'Like I said,' Pietro drawled. 'Throwing a lamb to the wolves... And you thought that I should just stop, park the car and let you walk right into the middle of it?'

How did he manage to do that? Marina wondered. How did he manage to wrong-foot her so easily, leaving her feeling gauche and naive, like some fish very much out of water, gasping for breath in the alien air of his world that was so very, very different from her own.

That made her still again as another even more disturbing thought came to her. One she should have considered before but hadn't actually done so.

'Did they hound you like this before—when I left?'

This time the look he turned on her was cool with cynicism.

'What did you expect?'

Marina wasn't sure if it was the bleakness of his tone or her own memories that made her shiver. She knew how the papers and celebrity magazines had been fascinated by their relationship, the hasty marriage. And she also couldn't forget the way that, whatever else he had done, Pietro had always done his very best to protect her from the prying lenses, the intrusive questions.

'I'm sorry.'

She could barely manage it through the sudden thickness in her throat. She knew how hard he fought to keep his personal life private, how he had always hated the way that the press intruded into everything he did. He must have loathed the blazing spotlight that her flight from their marriage had brought to focus on it even more.

'For bringing them to my door? They would have been here anyway.'

'Not just for that. But for never thanking you for the way you took them on when I miscarried—and again when I left.'

She knew only too well that her unexpectedly gentle treatment at the time had been a result of Pietro making a careful statement to the press and so drawing attention to himself instead of her. Then he had placed himself like a shield between her and the paparazzi, acting, in public at least, like the concerned husband he wasn't in private. He had always known how to put on the public mask, the one that spending so long in the celebrity columns had taught him to wear as second nature.

So the curious reporters, the persistent paparazzi, saw only the brutal control, the calm front he presented to them. Not that it was very much different behind the walls of the *castello*. He had been so emotionless, so unresponsive, that she had felt like kicking out at him. Anything to make him react. To have him say that he was at least disappointed.

When she'd challenged him with that at the time, he'd turned to her, face blank, eyes opaque.

'Disappointed?' he'd returned. 'Hell, yes, I'm disappointed. I thought there was going to be an heir to the estate.'

'And that's all? That's all you care about?'

'No.' He'd shaken his dark head, totally closed off from her. 'I'm disappointed that we have ended up in this situation when we could have waited—I should have waited.'

She should have held back, should never have asked the question. But she hadn't been able to bite her tongue, and so she had blurted it out.

'Why didn't you wait?'

'Is it not obvious? You were pregnant. If we had waited much longer, the world would have known. It was damage limitation.'

Something had died inside her then. Some part of her heart had closed off and she had shut herself away, hiding in her room to protect herself from the pain. Her actions had driven Pietro even further from her. He hadn't even troubled to hide it. And she hadn't been able to bring herself to care.

'If they get wind of the divorce now,' Pietro warned her, 'then they will be like hounds after a rat and will delight in hunting down any sordid, dirty detail they can find.'

'Why now? I mean...'

She couldn't finish the sentence but the quick, flashing glance Pietro turned on her held no question in it. His

immediate response showed that he had understood exactly
what she had not been able to say.

'Why ask for a divorce now? Is it not obvious?'

Not to me. She shook her head roughly, still having
trouble with the words, and she tried to focus her eyes hard
on the view beyond the windscreen where the buildings
were now thinning out; the outskirts of Palermo giving
way to the green of the countryside. She was afraid that if
she let him see her face he would read in her expression
the memory of all the days she had waited and hoped. The
long hours when she had dreamed, yearned—prayed—that
in spite of everything Pietro would come after her. That he
would come to find her and…

No. Desperately she pushed the weak thoughts aside.
Pietro had never come for her. Had never made contact
except for that one cold-blooded phone call, the one where
he had said—had demanded—that she come back to Sicily
now to talk about their marriage. That if she didn't then he
would know what to think.

'It seemed like the right time. I have duties to the
family—the estate. I still need to provide an heir and
my mother would like to be a *nonna* before she is much
older.'

'To a grandchild with a mother she can approve of,'
Marina added with a touch of bitterness.

A sidelong glance at the man at her side told her that he
was well aware of the significance of her remark.

'My mother only felt that way because she believed that
you had trapped me into marriage. I pointed out to her that
it takes two to make a baby.'

Unexpectedly and uncharacteristically, Pietro misjudged
the change of gears and the resulting crunching sound made
Marina jump. But he adjusted the movement swiftly and
steered the vehicle round another steep curve.

'She would have come round in time—if the child had been born.'

Another person who had felt that she would have been acceptable if only she had produced that important D'Inzeo heir, Marina reflected. Pietro's mother had not been an easy woman to get to know, and when Marina had lost the baby the older woman had withdrawn from her and had barely spoken.

'Does she have a suitable candidate in mind?'

'Several,' Pietro told her dryly, his mouth twisting on the word. 'Marriage to one of them will almost console her for the fact that my first marriage is ending in divorce.'

Marina winced sharply at the stab of pain his words inflicted on her. 'My first marriage': that was her summed up and dismissed in one short phrase. Done and dusted, put to one side.

'It's—not quite two years,' she managed, wincing at the roughness of her voice. 'I would have thought that...'

'That what?' Pietro prompted when her voice failed her.

'That you only had to wait another couple of months and we could have been divorced quietly and quickly—no blame—because we had been separated for two years. I would have thought that would be easier.'

'I thought you wanted your freedom,' Pietro said unexpectedly, startling her into turning to face him, to look him in the eye and try to read there just what he meant.

There was nothing there to help her. Nothing but the brief cold, clear stare of a man in total control. A man who had thought things out, decided on a plan of action and was determined to see it through. And something in the coolness of that stare gave her the disturbing feeling that, in spite of her earlier conviction that she had thrown him off-balance, she had in fact somehow played right into his hands.

'My freedom?'

He'd said that twice and she hadn't understood what lay behind it.

'You—you thought…?'

'That you wanted to move on. I also happen to believe that it is best to dispose of one spouse before considering another.'

'One spouse? Before considering… Stuart!'

How did he know about Stuart? She barely even considered him to be part of her life herself, yet…

'Have you been having me watched?'

Pietro made no response either to deny or agree, but the eyes that were fixed on the road ahead narrowed sharply in a way that was more than what was needed to concentrate on his driving.

'Is that what all this is about? Because you think that I have some new man in my life, you're…?'

The sudden thought that she might actually have to use the word 'jealous' to describe Pietro's reaction brought her up sharp. But no—to be jealous, you had to feel something. And what Pietro felt would only be a dark possessiveness and a strong concern for the D'Inzeo good name, not wanting it to be dragged through the mud by her new relationship.

'I have no intention of marrying Stuart—so if that was what was behind this sudden rush to divorce then you needn't have worried. You could have waited another few months and we could have had the divorce quickly and quietly on the grounds of two years' separation.'

'I did not want to wait another few months.'

Well, she'd asked for that. She had practically lain down and begged him to tell her that he couldn't wait to divorce, to be free of her. It was only what she had been claiming all the time she had been here.

'I do not wish to drift towards a divorce without thought, without making a decision. What is that the poet says? Not with a bang but with—'

'A whimper,' Marina finished for him when he left the sentence hanging.

She had the unnerving feeling that there was something she was missing, but for the life of her she couldn't begin to think what it was. It sounded almost as if Pietro had not been quite so hell-bent on a divorce as she had first thought. But in that case why summon her here like this?

Because he had heard about Stuart? He hadn't denied the accusation of having her watched, and now that she thought about it she recalled something he had said back in Matteo's office when the lawyer had been detailing the conditions set out in the divorce papers.

'And can you say the same for your boyfriend?' Pietro had demanded, hard and sharp. She hadn't taken much notice of it at the time, her mind too much on other things, but now she found herself taking out the memory and looking at it in a very different light.

Had the news of Stuart's place in her life really been the trigger that had pushed her husband into declaring that he wanted to bring their marriage to a formal end?

'What do you mean, a whimper?' she asked carefully.

'I believe that something as important as the ending of a marriage should be decided on rationally and talked out face to face by the two people involved.'

'And that justifies you kidnapping me like this?' she said, the words uneven as she struggled with the possible implications of that thought.

'I haven't kidnapped you. You came of your own free will.'

'Hardly *free*—you bullied me into doing as you wanted. But you can't just ride rough-shod all over me and expect me to like it!'

'Oh, I don't expect you to *like* it.'

There was laughter in Pietro's response but it was a dark, dangerous amusement, nothing close to real warmth at all.

'I know you too well for that. But you are the one who changed all the terms on which we were negotiating. You did not want the lawyers involved, so you left me no choice. And I did not bully you.'

'Oh, so does "bully" mean something else entirely in Sicilian?' Marina asked sarcastically. 'Something like "gently persuasive" or perhaps "carefully considerate"? Because, in English, being locked in a car with a man you never want to see again, and driven who knows where without your consent amounts to bullying in my book. You know that I expected to be in my hotel.'

'And I knew that you would probably use that as an excuse to dodge the discussion that we need to have. Hotels have doors and keys. I have always had a strong aversion to having one slammed and locked right in my face.'

He definitely knew her too well, Marina acknowledged inwardly. Either that or she had somehow given away the fact that that had been her plan all along—to escape to her room in the hotel and lock the door firmly against him. Only then would she have felt safe from his dangerously seductive presence, free from the sexual strings he seemed to be able to coil round her simply by existing.

Sitting here like this, so close to him in the confines of the car, was like being in the dry heat of a sauna in spite of the rain still coming down outside. The clean masculine scent of Pietro's body made her nostrils flare in sensual response and every movement he made, whether steering the powerful vehicle or changing gear, made the muscles in his strong back shift and slide under his clothes in a way that tugged on every nerve she possessed. Etched against the window, his strong profile with its olive skin and the straight slash of his nose looked as if it should have been the face of an emperor found on some Roman coin, unchanged over all the centuries.

But there had been an extra emphasis on that comment about doors that made it tug uncomfortably on her conscience, knowing how she had used that as a defence mechanism in the past.

'So is there any point in asking where we're going?'

'Somewhere where we can be a lot more comfortable—and a lot more private.'

That sent a shiver running down Marina's spine, making her feel as if one of the raindrops that was sliding down the windows had dropped down between her collar and her neck and was slowly, icily slithering down her back.

'Which tells me precisely nothing.'

'You'll find out when we get there. In the meantime, why don't you relax and enjoy the drive?'

'Relaxed is the exact opposite of the way I'm feeling.'

Again Pietro laughed, and this time there was a warmth in the sound that tugged at her heart and made the same tears that had stung her when she had thought of his kiss push at the backs of her eyes.

'No more questions,' he said. 'You will find out soon enough.'

'In other words, shut up and do as you are told. Well, that's fine by me. I'm not saying another word until I find out exactly where it is we're headed.'

Pietro's smile of wry acknowledgement almost had her breaking her word right at the start, particularly when she registered the direction they were taking. He was heading for the coast, she realised, and a sudden, shaken thud of her heart had her fearing that he might be heading home—driving towards the Castello D'Inzeo—the huge seventeenth-century house surrounded by vineyards and olive groves that had been home to his family for generations.

And the place where he had brought her as his bride less than three short years before.

She couldn't bear it, she told herself. He couldn't be so cruel. How could he take her to the place where she had once been so happy? The home that they had shared for the brief months of their passionate marriage?

Correction—the home where she had *believed herself* to be so happy, she amended bitterly. She had thought she was loved and had been dreafully deceived. Harsh reality had soon disabused her of the dreams her innocence had built around her naive, trusting heart.

They had left the city now and were speeding down the coast road with the blue, blue Thyrrhenian sea spread out before them. Marina's heart gave a little kick of distress as she recalled the spontaneous cry of joy she hadn't been able to hold back the very first time that they had rounded a curve in the road and she had seen the jewel-bright ocean spread out before them, the white foaming crests of the waves sparkling in the sunlight. She'd seen it then as a symbol of the brilliant, beautiful future that lay ahead of her.

Now she had to acknowledge how that thought had been as much of an illusion as the fact that the cool, colourless water had managed to look so like a sparkling aquamarine jewel. An unexpected return to the *palazzo* from a trip home to England a day earlier than she had been expected had shown her that. Fired with a new resolution that things were going to be so different, and desperate to be reunited with her husband, to ask him to start again, she had hurried to seek him out.

Only to find that he wasn't there. That he had left on an 'important business trip' and, so the curt note he had left behind informed her, he didn't plan to be home for at least ten days. Perhaps she could take the time to think about their marriage and where they went from here. If anywhere.

She hadn't needed ten days or anything like it. She had turned and run out of there before she could give in to the violent nausea roiling inside her stomach. Turned and fled back the way she had come, flinging herself into her car and driving away at top speed down the wide, curving drive as if all the hounds of hell were after her. She hadn't stopped until she had reached the airport where she had snatched at the first flight to London that was available, fleeing home, unable to settle until she had put hundreds of miles between herself and her uncaring, unloving husband.

She hadn't been back since. She hadn't even been able to bear to think of the place.

And the thought that Pietro might be taking her to the *palazzo* for his 'private' and 'comfortable' talk brought a bitter taste into her mouth, so that she feared she might actually be ill.

Pietro… Please… The words sounded in her head but she couldn't get them on to her tongue to actually speak them.

The turning for the *palazzo* came up on the left and she tensed apprehensively. But Pietro drove straight past, his attention still focused straight ahead.

The sense of relief was so great it was almost like a blow to her heart, making her breath escape in a rush, as with a deep sigh she subsided back in her seat.

Not the *palazzo*, then. But, if not the *palazzo*, then where?

Some time later, she had her answer. As the road climbed to a high point, with a sheer cliff on one side falling right down to the sea, Pietro slowed the car, indicated and turned down a steep, rutted road, heading towards the shore.

That was when she knew exactly where they were heading. And that it was worse, so much worse, than being taken to the *palazzo*.

CHAPTER SIX

THE cottage was exactly as she remembered it. Small and single-floored, it stood in the middle of vineyards, exotic cacti and fig and olive trees. On three sides of the property was a large terrace, partly covered, so that inside and out became one. It had a beautiful view of the strikingly large, arched bridge at the beginning of the valley of San Cataldo that opened out below it.

The house itself was painted an unexpected and uncompromising pink, so much so that Marina had laughed out loud at seeing it the first time when they had arrived at the cottage, Casalina, on their honeymoon.

'What are we doing here?'

The tangled feelings that had knotted in her throat made the words come out in a strangled gasp, one that had her wishing she could control herself better and not give so much away.

Pietro barely spared her a glance as he steered the car into the small courtyard and brought it to a smooth halt.

How could he be so heartless as to bring her here, to the tiny isolated cottage where they had spent the seven magical days of their honeymoon?

For one short week she had lived an idyll of joy and innocence. It had all been so totally perfect. She had been crazily in love with her brand-new husband and had believed that he felt the same about her. It was only when they had moved to the spectacular surroundings of the *palazzo*, and the sophisticated way of life that Pietro knew there, that she had realised how naive she was to think that the week in Casalina had been anything like the reality she could look forward to.

'I said I wanted somewhere quiet.'

Well, it was that—too quiet, as far as Marina was concerned. Quiet might have made for perfection when she had been alone with him before. When all she had wanted was to be with Pietro, revel in his company, enjoy his conversation and indulge in the untamed sensuality of his lovemaking. Then, being alone with him had been a glorious thing, each day pure joy from start to finish. Now it was something to dread, to anticipate with a terrible sense of foreboding, like a dark thundercloud looming on the horizon bringing with it the threat of dangerous weather.

'Are you coming in?' he asked her now, striding into the small house as if all the memories that were swirling round her, tugging at her nerves and twisting her heart in pain, meant nothing at all to him.

But then, of course, that was probably exactly how he felt. There would be no distress in his thoughts of their honeymoon, the time spent at Casalina together, because he had never suffered from the foolish, romantic delusions that had held her in their grip. He had never thought that all his dreams had come true—in fact she doubted if he had ever dreamed of anything in his life.

Except perhaps the heir he had thought that she was going to provide him with. The baby that had still been alive, still growing inside her, when she had first arrived at Casalina.

Her heart lurched, her throat closing on a sound that

was almost a sob no matter how hard she tried to hold it back.

She couldn't go into the cottage, not with him, not now, not with all the hurts of the past coming between them. Yet what choice did she have? As she hesitated on the threshold, her eyes went to where the car stood, still with the key in the ignition. For a moment she was tempted to dash back to the vehicle, pull open the door and slide into the driving seat. She could put her foot down, get out of here and then…

Her thoughts slid to a halt. And then what?

Where could she go? What would she do? The thought of facing the busy traffic of Palermo's streets made her stomach quiver sharply on something close to panic. And, if she did manage to find her way back to the hotel, she would only be walking straight into the ambush set by the paparazzi who had been hanging about outside. Straight from the frying pan into the fire. And right now she didn't know if she'd rather face Pietro and his 'quiet and private talk' or the fearsome pressures of the press, the flash of their camera bulbs, the fierce thrust of their microphones in her face.

Drawing in a deep breath, she forced herself to follow him inside the cottage, fighting the ache of memories that every step awakened.

The cottage really was tiny, just a single open-plan room with a kitchen at one side, the doors to the bedroom and bathroom leading off it. It hadn't been changed or even redecorated since she had last been there. The polished wooden floor, painted furniture and red-cushioned settee brought back so many emotions in a rush that for a moment she actually staggered, unsteady, on her feet.

'You OK?' Pietro had spotted her reaction, and his head turned sharply in her direction.

'I'm fine.'

She suspected that the smile with which she accompanied the words was rather too much. Too wide, too bright. Too obviously false. So she covered it with a hasty explanation.

'It's a bit dark in here after the sunlight.'

She didn't need Pietro's cynical-eyed glance out of the window, where the weak sun was struggling through the still-cloudy sky, to tell her that she hadn't convinced him at all. The door to the bedroom stood slightly ajar, she noticed, the space it left revealing the wide, king-sized bed, totally unexpected in a tiny house like this. She didn't want to remember that bed or the images that were sparked off inside her unwilling head simply by the briefest glimpse of it.

'Why did you bring me here?' she asked and heard his breath hiss in through his teeth in a sound of impatient irritation.

'You know why. The paparazzi.'

'That isn't what I meant.'

'No?'

She had his attention now. And she didn't know if she was glad of the fact that at least he was listening intently to her or if she wished that she hadn't made him focus on her quite so closely. The living room of the cottage was so small, so compact, that his powerful form seemed to be exaggerated in its lean height and strength. His dark head was turned towards her, burning eyes fixed on her face, and his broad, straight shoulders seemed to block out all the daylight, bringing an ominous shadow into the room.

'No, what I meant was why did you bring me here *then*? When we were first married? Why bring me to a tiny place like this when there was that huge *castello* just a few miles away—the perfect place for a honeymoon?'

Why *had* he brought her here? Pietro asked himself. 'Why' seemed to be the word that had been swinging round and round in his head so much since the moment Marina had walked into his lawyer's room and back into his life.

Why had he ever married her? Why had he decided that now was the time to divorce her? Why had he felt the need to bring his brand-new bride to Casalina for their honeymoon instead of taking her straight to the luxury of the *castello*?

'If you must know, I thought that you could get to know the real Sicily. A place of beauty where the way of life is simple and basic. Where the lemons ripen in the groves, and often the only movement during the day is when the shepherd's family who live higher up the valley drive their flock to the mountains early in the morning, wandering back when the sun begins to set.'

Maledizione, that was only part of the answer, though he hated to admit it. Admitting it meant that he would have to acknowledge he had had his doubts even then, even in the first days of their marriage. Life, and one too many bad experiences, had taught him to be wary. He knew from bitter reality how often women were attracted to his money, his position, and not to the man himself. So he had brought Marina here because he had wanted to see the truth. To see her response to the reality of the simplest style of Sicilian life instead of the wealth that belonged to his family.

He had had second thoughts even before they had settled in his home. He had known that they had rushed into marriage, that the heat and hunger of their sexual passion had scrambled his brain and had him thinking with far more basic parts of his anatomy. So he had brought her here as a sort of a test, the result of which he had believed would show him the truth behind the enticing sexual façade. One hesitation, one blink of disappointment, and he would have known the truth.

'I thought you enjoyed our honeymoon here.'

If she hadn't, he would have played things much more carefully, watched her more closely. But she had shown such enthusiasm for the cottage, and the countryside around it, that he had relaxed his scrutiny, let down his guard.

'Oh, I did. I loved it here. But I never understood why you did things that way.'

'I thought it was better to be safe than sorry.'

He might as well tell her the truth now. There was no reason to hold back, no point in concealing anything from her.

'I had been disillusioned in the past. What is it that you say? One bite…'

'Once bitten, twice shy,' Marina supplied automatically, her tone odd, her expression distracted—much as he expected his own face would look if he could see it.

'And I did not think that it was fair to force you to spend your honeymoon in the same house as your mother-in-law.'

'Particularly not a mother-in-law who really wanted a pure-bred Sicilian wife for you. She never really forgave me for being English. Or for not giving you the heir you needed.'

She was wandering round the room, trailing her fingers over the backs of the chairs, along the blue-painted surface of the cupboard against the wall. As he watched he was taken back to those early days of their marriage, to a time when it had seemed to him that a new dawn had broken in his life. That a new era of trust and peace—and, damn it, happiness—had formed. She had wandered around the room in much the same way then, though she had had a very different expression on her face. A half-smiling, half-dream-like look that had made her appear so wonderfully young and innocent. So lovable.

He had actually allowed himself to hope that this marriage could really be for ever. The sort of 'for ever' he had never really believed in before—not with the evidence of his parents' war-zone of a relationship before him. An arranged marriage between two important families, their marriage had barely lasted as long as his own. No sooner had the all-important heir—Pietro himself—been born than the marriage had crashed and burned with husband and wife living entirely separate lives.

But Marina had seemed so different, so fresh, so innocent. He had been totally unprepared for the disillusionment when it had come.

Just as he recalled why he had played things so carefully in the beginning, so he now remembered the force and determination with which she had thrown the divorce papers in his face and her ardent declaration that she wanted nothing from him. He had been so wrong to have suspicions about her only having married him for his money. So, then, what did she truly want from him?

'Did you really not read the divorce papers through?'

When she turned to face him, her green eyes were strangely opaque, all expression under control so that it was like looking at a mask. A carved, motionless veneer covered her features. It was a sight that took him back into bitter memories of their marriage.

'No, I didn't. Why would I?'

'I was going to give you this place.'

Immediately he could see it in the change in her face. Her expression suddenly altered, the mask slipped, and he caught sight of a very different person underneath.

At last he'd got through to her. At last he'd pushed her to reveal something she'd been determined to keep hidden.

And what had flashed into her eyes in that moment had showed him a very different side to her. It was as if the years in between had suddenly been stripped away and she was once more the woman he had first met.

Had she really looked so much younger? She had only been twenty-two, he reminded himself. He had never really thought about how young that was.

She had seemed so alive then, so vivid and bright, like a butterfly. Like the woman who had walked into Matteo's office, not the pinched-faced, remote, unwelcoming wife she had become at the end of their marriage.

'Why?' Marina asked. She'd got herself back under control but there was still a faint quaver in her voice that he caught, attuned to her as he was, before she clamped down hard on it again. 'Why would you do that?'

Why?

He didn't have an answer to that except the one that had been uppermost in his thoughts when he had been discussing the details of the divorce with Matteo. His lawyer had told him in no uncertain terms that his reasons for putting Casalina into the settlement at all were stupid to the point of crazy, but he hadn't listened.

'Because you loved it.'

'Because...'

Marina felt as if her rational mind had suddenly fused, blinked off, leaving her in total darkness for a moment. Then when it came back on again it was as if everything had changed and she was in a world she had never inhabited before. A world where nothing really made sense.

Because you loved it.

So why tell her now? Why let her know that the cottage had been part of the divorce settlement that he had been prepared to give her? Was this a test, to see if he could get her to change her mind, alter her tactics? She couldn't answer that; she only knew that in the moment he had told her he had been prepared to give her Casalina she had temporarily lost her grip on the control that was so vital to her seeing through this difficult time with any degree of success and composure. Just for the space of a couple of uneven heartbeats, she had been unable to hold back on the rush of emotion that had swamped her, the terrible, slashing need that had torn at her heart.

'How can you say that?'

The words felt as if they had been torn from her, ripping their way up her throat, so that she felt they should emerge splattered with drops of blood.

'How could you be so cruel?'

'Cruel?'

If she had lashed out with her hands instead of her words, and slapped him hard in the face, she couldn't have had more of a dramatic effect. Pietro actually took a step backwards, flinging up his head, pale eyes clashing with hers.

'What?'

If she had to explain, she knew it would finish her. The darkness was there in her mind, reaching out to enclose her, but if she put it into words it would take a whole new form—one that had almost destroyed her once before. But, even as she struggled with the pain of her thoughts, she saw colour leach from Pietro's face, saw the shock of realisation darken his eyes.

'Cruel,' he muttered again but with a totally different intonation. 'Oh hell, Marina, I'm sorry.'

'Sorry?' She couldn't believe she had heard right.

'I never thought—*dannazione*—I should have thought! I should never have brought you here when it was obvious that you... That the whole place would be filled with memories of the baby.'

Of the baby…

It was something but it wasn't enough. And the fact that he only saw one reason for caring, for feeling that he had made a mistake in bringing her here when everything else was so much more complicated, seemed to force a cruel hand into her chest, grab hold of her heart and twist it cruelly, squeezing until all the life was crushed out of it.

'You weren't so damn concerned when it happened.'

The words weren't truly accurate, and the unfairness was bound to hurt. But right now she wasn't thinking about being fair, only about lancing the viciously throbbing sore where all her memories lay just below the surface, covered over but not healed. Opening it meant letting out the poison of her thoughts that had been festering in the years since she had walked out on her marriage. The anguish of release had something of the same effect as a rush of powerful spirit straight to her head, making it spin wildly.

'Of course I was concerned…'

She heard Pietro's voice as if it came from a long way away, muffled and blurred by the dark, throbbing clouds inside her head.

'Oh yes, you were disappointed.'

'You bet I was disappointed—I wanted that baby every bit as much—'

'No!'

It was a painful gasp that she could barely get out, feeling it strangled deep inside her throat, knotted tight on its way into the open.

'No, don't say that!' She shook her head violently, feeling strands of her hair lash her face as they whirled around her head. 'Don't say that you did.'

How could he tell her he had wanted the baby every bit as much as she had, when she had loved the child because it was *his* as well as for itself. Because it was a part of the man she had come to adore so fervently, so fast. When she had lost the baby she had lost Pietro as well.

Acid tears burned in her eyes, blinding her, making it impossible to see him as anything other than a black, looming shape somewhere in front of her. But was he close or far away? She had no way of knowing until she felt the touch of something on her hand. Something warm and soft, barely there, but a gentle contact that shattered what was left of the barriers she had built up around her, taking with them what little was left of her self-control.

'Marina...'

'No!'

She was whirling, spinning on her heel, seeking sightlessly for the door to leave the cottage. To get out, and away from her memories, away from her feelings. But even as she tried to take a step forward, to take flight, the gentle touch on her hand moved to her wrist, tightened, became stronger and held her back. The pressure caught her up and swung her back, so that she came up hard against the warm, strong shape, the solidity of ribcage, the heat of skin and muscle that was all Pietro.

'No,' he said, his tone harsh and rasping, cutting through the fog that swirled inside her head. 'No, you cannot hide behind locked doors this time. Or run away from me. You walked out on me once before and never came back. I have no intention of letting that happen again.'

'You can't stop me. I won't let you stop me. You have no right.'

'I have every right.' It was obdurate, unyielding, and it felt like a blow to her bruised and aching head. 'You gave me that right on our wedding day and you have never taken it away. I am still your husband.'

'In name only.'

'And the father of our child.'

But that was a step too far, one wound too many on her already bleeding soul.

'Don't say that! Don't say it! I lost my baby. You lost the heir you wanted!'

'And that meant that I couldn't love him or her?' Pietro's voice was filled with dark challenge, one that was mirrored in his eyes.

A challenge that she knew she couldn't meet.

'I know for sure that you never loved *me*. Never!'

Finding a strength she hadn't known she possessed, she wrenched her hand from Pietro's grip and launched herself at him blindly, arms flailing, fingers clenched. She sensed rather than saw the one jerky movement with which Pietro took his head back and out of range, but after that he simply stood there and let her react. He let her pound her fists against the hardness of his chest, thudding them wildly, furiously, desperately on to the powerful bone, strong muscles and warm skin.

'You only loved what I could give you!'

For the space of a few lost seconds she was out of control, lashing at him, at herself, at her memories. Losing herself and finding release in the same wild heartbeats. But then at last the blind despair finally burned itself out. Something broke inside her and, as if a wire that had held her upright suddenly snapped, she collapsed against him, abandoning herself to the gasping, choking sobs that would not could not be held back.

Pietro simply let her cry. At first he held himself tight and stiff, totally unconnected. But then, as the storm of her tears took the strength from her body, his arms came round her and held her in a way that was both comforting and supportive. And, inside the cocoon of their warmth, in an instinctive movement of a small creature seeking the protection of its home, Marina turned her face into his shoulder and wept.

She had no idea how long they stayed like that, Pietro silent, still, herself a molten wreck. But at long last the sobs slowed, eased, ceased. The last one fell into the silent room on a final sigh and, sniffing inelegantly, she dashed a hand to her cheeks, wiping away the tears, not daring to look up into Pietro's face. Just for a second she felt something brush her hair. She didn't know if it was his fingers or his cheek resting against her head. And then, still without a word, he moved, easing her from him and across to the red settee, settling her down on the cushions before he reached for a box of tissues on the dresser nearby.

Carefully he wiped the moisture from her skin, repairing the damage that the storm of weeping had inflicted. Her mascara had run, streaking her skin, and some of the tissues that he tossed into the bin were black with it. All the time he never said a word until at last, eyes narrowed in careful assessment, he looked into her face, checking out his handiwork, perhaps searching for something else as well. Something that had her dodging away, dropping her own gaze in discomfort to stare at the polished wooden floor.

As if the movement had freed something in him, Pietro pushed himself to his feet, swinging away and crossing the room. He walked to the window, then back again, coming to stand beside the sofa. He towered over her, feet in the polished hand-made shoes planted firmly, wide apart, hands pushed deep into the pockets of his trousers. Glancing up between eyelashes still spiked with tears, she could see how the fabric bunched over his tight fists, revealing the control he was imposing on himself, the effort he was putting into it.

'You can say…' He spoke at last, his voice rough edged

and harsh. 'You can accuse me of not having loved you enough. You can tell me that I never loved you at all. But you will never, *never*, accuse me of not wanting, not loving, my child.'

It was a statement, not a question. He didn't seem to need an answer but there was such intensity in his voice, such total conviction, that she could make no response. She managed a silent, blurry-eyed nod, not knowing whether he actually saw it or not.

'The day you lost the baby,' Pietro went on above her head, 'was one of the worst days of my life.'

Same here… And so much more. But a disturbing thickness in Pietro's voice—the words sounding as if they were coming unravelled at the edges—struck home like the stinging flick of a whip. Lost in her own misery, trapped by the terrible sense of desolation, had she spared a thought for what Pietro had been feeling too? He had wanted an heir but he had also lost a child.

'I'm sorry I f-failed you…'

'Failed?'

Another different tone, a bewildering one this time. Her mind was too numbed, too bruised, to catch up with the swift changes of mood that seemed to happen as often as she blinked.

'*Failed.*'

Hard hands came down to clamp around her arms, hauling her up out of her seat until she was face to face with him, green eyes locking with pale blue in a face that suddenly seemed to have lost the glow from its natural tan and was all planes and angles, the skin appearing drawn tight over his cheekbones.

'And how the hell did you fail me?'

'I lost…'

But Pietro wouldn't let her finish.

'*You* are not the only person involved here. We made that baby together. The only failure here is that we did not lose it together.'

'No, we were already coming apart at the seams before then.'

The bitterness of her memories made her say it, but even as she felt the words leave her lips she knew that in spite of everything her heart had lifted irresistibly at the thought that at least he didn't blame her for the loss of the baby. She had blamed herself enough at the time. She had felt useless and a failure for not being able to give him the heir he wanted so much.

'You didn't even want me any more.'

'You were pregnant!'

And swollen. And tired. And there had been no such thing as morning sickness—all-day sickness, every day… She should have seen that as a warning sign, but she had been struggling to keep her head above water as it was.

'Not exactly the perfect *principessa* you were looking for.'

'I knew you were pregnant when I married you. I was proud to see how you changed—to know that my child was growing within you. Nothing else mattered.'

'And was that why you moved into another room—for the baby's sake?'

Something had changed again. The mood that had pushed him to reassure her that she hadn't failed had darkened, bringing his black brows together in a frown.

'I would have done anything that meant our child stayed healthy. You were uncomfortable, nauseous, not sleeping well.'

She would have slept better if she had had his arms around her, with his body curved protectively around hers.

From the moment she had set foot in the grand *palazzo*

and seen the reality of the huge estate, the power and wealth that her baby would be heir to, she had felt out of her depth and totally lost. The fact that Pietro had immediately seemed to be swallowed up in the details of running that estate had left her feeling even more vulnerable and inadequate. Even his mother had been totally absent.

But she hadn't been able to admit to that then, and here and now it was an admission too far, especially to a man who had just acknowledged that his concern had been for his unborn child.

The fact that that still burned so cruelly warned her that it was no longer the past she should be worrying about. The real cause for concern was the way the past had leached into the present, finding the small but dangerously vulnerable chink in the armour she had tried to build around herself. It had weaselled its way inside, opening that armour up and leaving her more dangerously exposed than ever before.

There is nothing I could want from you, she had told him. *Nothing at all.*

Even as the words had left her lips she should have known them for the lie they were.

She had once wanted so much—wanted his love, his devotion, his heart. And, when she had learned that he didn't have any such thing to give her, something had shrivelled in her own heart, splitting it apart until she had thought that she would die from the pain of it. That was when she had known that she had to get out. Get away and never ever look back. Looking back was fatal—even more so was *coming* back. Setting foot on Sicily again was like stepping right into the lion's den.

And the worrying thing was that she knew that in the last few minutes she had been unable to hide it. She had given him an insight into the fact that she was not armoured enough against him and the memories he awoke in her.

She had let him see deeper into her heart than was safe. Deeper even than she had understood herself. And she had no idea how he might use the knowledge she had given him.

CHAPTER SEVEN

'This talking thing...'

Marina forced her voice into as casual a tone as she could manage and made herself stroll over to the window as she spoke, praying that her unsteady legs would hold her. Once safely across the room, she could at least rest a hand against the wall for support and focus her eyes on the view outside, the wider terrace and the valley beyond, and avoid having to look into Pietro's watching face and see the sharp observation in his eyes.

She needed to get the conversation onto safer ground. Ground that would mean she could stick to her original plan of getting out of here and home again as fast as she could. With every second that passed she was letting him more and more into the heart that she had vowed would be armoured against him this time. With every beat of that heart he was breaching her defences, finding chinks in that armour. And that was far, far too dangerous to be allowed to continue.

'Discussing terms. Don't you think we'd better get on with it? After all, I do have a plane to catch if I'm to get home. And I wouldn't want to miss my flight.'

'You don't have a flight to miss,' Pietro reminded her dryly from behind her in the room. 'The jet is mine and you can travel whenever you want.'

Whenever *he* wanted was the truth, Marina reflected bitterly. He gave the orders and the pilot would obey them. Which meant that she was practically a prisoner until Pietro decided she could go.

'All the same, I don't think there's really anything to discuss.'

'Not about the divorce, perhaps, but our marriage is a very different matter. But I think that perhaps it is time that we ate.'

'Ate?' Marina knew that her disbelief rang in her voice. They were talking about the break-up of their marriage and he wanted to think about *food*?

'It is well after one.' Pietro had come to stand behind her. She could almost feel the heat of his body reaching out to enclose her, the scent of his skin setting sensitive nerves jangling in uncontrolled response. 'And I for one am ravenous. I am sure that you must be too.'

'I...' Marina began, but even as she spoke her stomach growled sharply, revealing the denial she had been about to make as a lie. The soft sound of Pietro's laughter behind her had her whirling round to face him, regretting it as soon as she saw the way amusement softened his hard face, putting a new light in the pale depths of his eyes.

'Have you eaten at all today?' he asked, jolting her with the revelation as to how well he knew the way her appetite deserted her when she was apprehensive. 'How about it, hmm, Marina?' he went on, not needing her answer. 'Some time out—no talk of divorce. I reckon you need it.'

The way he touched one finger to her cheek, smoothing the traces left by the storm of weeping, told her without words just what she looked like and why he had come to this decision. And she couldn't but be grateful to him for it.

'We both do. And the little *trattoria* down by the shore is still there…' he added enticingly.

She wanted to meet him halfway. Wanted the truce he seemed to be calling—the chance for time out. The truth was that she felt battered and emotionally bruised and would be grateful for a chance to recover and recoup.

'The one that makes the wonderful *pasta con le sarde*?' Memory had her mouth watering at just the name of the famous Palermitan dish of pasta with fresh sardines.

'The same.'

'But won't the paparazzi…?'

'They will still be hanging around the hotel, waiting for you. We could walk down now that the weather is improving…' As if to confirm his words, the last of the drizzle faded away and the sun came out from behind a cloud.

'I'm not exactly dressed.'

She knew she was prevaricating and Pietro didn't even trouble to answer. Heading into the bedroom, he opened up a wardrobe and the next moment a bundle of clothing was tossed onto the bed.

'There should be something here that would do.'

'My old clothes…'

The ones she had left here, when they had honeymooned in the cottage, and then abandoned when she had fled to England.

'Mine too.' Pietro pulled tee-shirt and jeans from the other side of the cupboard.

'But why have you kept them?'

He had already tossed aside the formal jacket he had worn to the lawyer's office, hands stilling on his shirt as he looked up and straight at her.

'I have not been here at all since you left.'

'Never?'

'Never.'

Which opened up as many questions as it answered—but clearly Pietro was not prepared to take things any further as he peeled off his shirt, dropping it on the bed too. The sight of the lean expanse of bronzed skin, the soft, dark hair hazing his chest, was enough to drive away all other thoughts from Marina's mind, freezing her where she stood. Memory brought back the feel of that golden skin under her fingertips, the brush of the black hairs against her breasts, making her heart clench and her mouth dry in remembered sensuality. It was only when his hands dropped to the leather belt around his waist, flicking the buckle undone, that she jolted herself into action, heading for the bathroom and the chance to change in privacy herself.

Removing the formal suit and blouse seemed disturbingly like emerging from the protective armour she had carefully put on to come to Sicily. And the loose turquoise shirt and white cotton cropped trousers Pietro handed her were the sort of casual wear she had never had the time or inclination to wear in her new life in England. They had belonged to a younger, more naive Marina.

A happier Marina.

That thought had her eyes opening wide, flying to the reflection of her face in the mirror over the basin. Her make-up was a mess, her face still bearing the marks of the tear storm, mascara smudges around her eyes and on her cheeks. But all the same—impossibly—she looked better than she had done for ages. There was a light in her eyes, and a wash of colour on her cheeks.

Was it possible that just the thought of time out spent with Pietro had put it there? The idea brought her hands to her cheeks, covering the revealing glow. But that only made the brightness of her eyes stand out more. Shockingly so.

'Be careful!' Marina told her reflection sternly. 'Be very, very careful.'

Even though her rational self spoke the warning words aloud, something inside her, something totally irrational, seemed to refuse to take them in. And when she turned towards the door to go back into the living room, having washed away the mascara smudges and the tearstains, the sudden skip of her heart warned her that she was risking heading into deep, deep waters.

But the really dangerous thing was that she just couldn't bring herself to care.

The sun was sinking down behind the far horizon by the time they returned to the cottage, bathing the tiny house in a burning glow, turning its pink walls crimson and gold. Seen like this it was a magical place, a dream, a place out of time. In just the same way, the afternoon she had spent with Pietro had truly been a time out away from the tension of the divorce negotiations, the pain of memories of the past. They had walked, talked—of safe, every-day topics—and they had shared a wonderful meal and a bottle of wine. She had enjoyed every minute of it. If there had been any moment, any small thing that had marred the peace now between them, it was the way that as they'd walked sometimes their hands would bump, touch, come so close. She had had to fight hard with herself to stop the instinctive movement to reach out and take hold of his hand, fold her fingers round his and walk together hand in hand. That freedom was not hers any more. And Pietro showed no sign at all of wanting to revive the once-familiar closeness.

Now as they walked back into the cottage she felt the shadows start to close around her once more—the shadows of reality rather than the gathering shadows of the evening that darkened the small rooms. The time out was over, the tiny idyll in the private battle they had been fighting was gone, and now she knew it would be back to skirmishing and duelling with words.

There was little point in delaying the inevitable any longer, so she pushed herself to be the first to broach the subject as soon as they were back inside the cottage.

'So what do we still need to sort out?'

The beauty of the trees and the landscape beyond the window started to blur as Marina forced herself to stare straight ahead and not risk turning to look at Pietro's face. She knew that the memory of his smile, his laughter, the way it had fizzed its way along every one of her nerves as he had sat opposite her in the small white-painted *trattoria*, would destroy her if she let herself dwell on it. Outside everything was still and silent apart from the swift, jerky movement of a bright green lizard that ran across the wall to the left and then disappeared into the worn stone.

'Because I really had hoped that I would be back home today with everything signed and sealed.'

The need to keep her defences up made her voice spiky and sharp. Behind her she heard Pietro's indrawn breath and the soft, slow sound of his footsteps on the polished wooden floor as he moved towards her. The subtle scent of that lime shampoo tantalised her nostrils, the undertones of clean, male skin sending pulses of heated response through her veins.

'And as there's nothing that I want from you...'

'Perhaps there was something I wanted you to give me.'

Pietro's response had a sting like the flick of a whip, making Marina spin round to face him. He was closer than she had anticipated—unnervingly so—and she found herself staring straight at a wide expanse of chest under the close-fitting black tee-shirt, the muscular length of arms exposed by the short sleeves tightening disturbingly as if working hard for restraint.

'To give *you*?'

Her instant response dried her throat so that to her fury her voice croaked betrayingly.

'Or perhaps I should say give *back*.'

'I have nothing of yours to give back.'

She brought her hands up in front of her to emphasise the words and it was the direction of his eyes towards the glint of gold on the left hand that gave her a much-needed clue.

'Oh—of course.' It was all she could manage as she fought against the pain that slashed through her.

How could she have been so stupid, so slow on the uptake? There was one obvious thing that Pietro would want back—two, if she counted the beautiful emerald and diamond engagement ring he had given her when she had accepted his proposal.

Refusing to allow herself to think about that for fear the memories of her happiness that day would destroy her, Marina tugged at her wedding ring with shaking fingers. It didn't want to move. Some appalling conspiracy between her body and her subconscious mind had made her finger swell so that the ring stuck right where it was.

'I'm sorry, it won't…'

Tears blurred her eyes so that she could barely see what she was doing. Nervous perspiration beaded her forehead, making her breathing uneven. She knew that hot colour had flooded her cheeks—she could feel the glow of it in her skin—and that only made everything so much worse. She could sense the burn of his eyes on her too, flaying off a vital protective layer, leaving her painfully vulnerable and exposed.

'I can't…' Fighting a sense of ridiculous panic, she tugged harder, twisting the ring, pulling…

'Oh, damn it—I can't—'

She broke off in shock and confusion as Pietro suddenly put out a hand, closing cool fingers over her own hot flustered ones.

'Marina, it's OK.'

His voice was calm, the tone as controlled as his touch, and she stilled underneath it, her blood seeming to freeze in shock.

'It *is* OK, Marina,' Pietro repeated, his voice deepening on the words. 'That isn't what I want.'

'But…'

She didn't dare to look up, to look into his face. There was something new in his mood; she could tell that from his tone, from the notes in it that resonated through her head, making her thoughts spin, her pulse thud.

And suddenly it was as if heat had raced through his veins so that his touch on her hand was no longer cool, no longer controlled. She felt the heat of his skin over hers, the hard strength of his fingers, muscle and bone. His touch had altered, the pressure of it no longer calming or soothing. Instead it had a sensual pressure, a hint of demand.

'Marina,' he said, softly, roughly; his thumb moved, stroking a sensual path over the back of her hand, one caressing sweep over her skin, then a pause and back again. Slow, enticing, seductive. Making her heart pound, her breath catch.

'Pietro…'

Hearing her own voice told her just what was happening to her. And it sent a shiver down her spine, one that she was unable to recognise. It was either fear or a quiver of excited anticipation and even she had no way of knowing which.

'Pietro, don't,' was what she had planned to say, what she thought she would say. But somehow the second word faded from her thoughts even as she tried to say it. Another stroke of that broad thumb, the pad slightly roughened by some physical work, had her heart kicking hard. The heat of his body seemed to surround her. She was so close she could see him draw in each breath, the movement of his chest not quite as steady as it had been just moments before.

Could it be that he was feeling every bit as shaken as she was?

When she nerved herself to lift her eyes to his, it was to discover that he was even closer than before. That his head was bent, his face inclined towards hers, so that all she had to do was lift her chin and their mouths would meet.

So close and then—nothing. So close and then he was waiting—for her to make the first move?

Her breath sighed from her throat, and she slicked her tongue nervously over desperately dry lips. The movement did very little to ease the tension she felt. If anything, it made it so much worse as she saw Pietro's darkened gaze drop to follow its nervous path. She saw his tanned throat move in a swift, convulsive swallow and knew there was no need for words to communicate how they were feeling. It was all there in the silence, in the heat that had nothing to do with the sunlight outside but was purely the result of the burning chemical reaction between them.

Still he held her hand, his grip hard and warm, and she knew that she couldn't bring herself to tug her fingers away. It was more than her stinging senses would allow.

'Pietro…' she managed on a very different note, her heart clenching as she heard the thread of encouragement and husky sensuality that ran through the sound.

Unable to stop herself, not knowing if it was safe, not

caring, she made the slight movement that was all that
was needed and brushed her mouth along the fullness of
his lower lip. Just the taste of him acted like the strongest
alcoholic spirit, the most potent of aphrodisiacs, and in a
rush of heated awareness she knew that one kiss, one taste,
was not enough.

It was obvious that Pietro thought the same. Her name
was a rough groan on his tongue before his mouth captured
hers in a bruising, hungry kiss that knocked her head back,
crushing her lips against her teeth. For the space of a couple
of shaken heartbeats she feared she might lose her foot-
ing, but then his hands freed hers, long fingers coming up
to spear into her hair, twisting in the silky strands as he
cupped the bones of her skull, holding her just where he
wanted so that he could deepen and prolong the kiss.

What little was left of rational thought in Marina's mind
was pushed out by the heated swirl of dark sensuality that
took over all her senses. She was lost in the taste of him,
the feel of him, the strength of him. Her hands were on his
arms, on his back, sliding over the clinging material of his
tee-shirt to stroke down the long, straight spine, down to
where the leather belt cinched his narrow waist. Against her
lips she heard his murmur of approving response and felt
him move close, crushing her up against the lean hardness
of his frame. The swollen evidence of his erection told of
his arousal, its heat and power pressed into the cradle of
her hips, making her shift from one foot to another. The
soft movement of her body against his brought a groan of
hungry response from his lips.

Lifted onto her toes, she found herself half-walked,
half-carried across the room until once again she had her
back against the wall. The pressure of it at her spine, and
the muscular power of the male body crushed along the
front of her, kept her upright as Pietro kissed her with such

erotic thoroughness that her head was spinning in heated delight.

'I don't damn well want your ring back,' he muttered, rough and thick against her lips, snatching hungry kisses between the words. His hands were tugging at the buttons on her top, his strong fingers in such a rush that they tore the fastenings open, sending a couple of the buttons spinning away to land on the wooden floor with a faint clatter a few feet away. 'The only thing in the world I want is you, with me, in my bed, underneath me—opening to me.'

The only thing in the world I want is you...

Was she really hearing right? Marina asked herself as the words swung round inside her head, hitting hard against what little was left of her ability to think. Did he really mean that all he wanted was her back in his life? That he didn't give a damn about the divorce?

Was it possible that...?

But then those urgent hands wrenched away the last of the cotton that covered her aching breasts and the feel of his hot palms against her yearning flesh sent her spinning away into a world of pure sensation. A place where nothing else mattered but the feel of his caresses, the thunder of hunger in every nerve. It was like opening the floodgates on the rush of liquid need that swept through her, impossible to control, impossible to hold back. Her mouth was ravenous under his, taking his kisses and giving them back with greedy, snatching haste. Her hands were as urgent as his, seeking the strength of him beneath his clothes. They pulled up his shirt, finding the warm satin flesh, the hard power of muscle underneath it.

Her sigh of contentment when she felt the reality of him was caught in his mouth and given back to her with the next yearning caress, making him swear in rough, hard Italian as he could not control his own response.

'*Madre de D…*'

She was swung off her feet, lifted and carried the short distance across the room to where the door to the bedroom stood ajar. Shouldering it open, Pietro carried her into the simply furnished room where wooden shutters closed the windows, making the bedroom cool and dark at the back of the house.

Just for one moment as he lowered her onto the bed, the sensation of the soft white cotton, the aroma of sunlight and lemon on the pillowcases, threw up a memory of the idyllic honeymoon they had once spent together in this place. But even as she fought against letting it take a grip Pietro had come down beside her, shrugging off his tee-shirt as he did so. The scent of his skin, touched from their time by the sea, the heat of it against her own exposed flesh, the taste of it under her mouth, was more than enough to drive away the lingering sadness and replace it with a fresh rush of need and excitement.

'This is what brought us together,' Pietro muttered against her neck as he stripped what remained of her clothes from her with the ease and efficiency of familiarity. 'And this is what will keep us close—not lawyers, not settlements, but the call of senses, the connection of man to woman, body to body…'

Naked now, he held her in his arms, letting her feel the heat of his body, the powerful pulse of his arousal nudging between her legs. Marina felt the moisture of need flood her, awakening the innermost core of her, preparing her for the intimate invasion that she knew was inevitable. She wanted it so much she felt she was dying by inches just having to wait. She was reaching for him clutching at him, pulling him closer, urging him on. He was hard and hot and full, just how she needed him to be with her, inside her, taking her. Driving her mindless with need and then appeasing that need in the way only he had ever been able to do.

His mouth was at her breast now, teasing the stiffened peaks of her nipples, alternately suckling hard, even grazing the sensitive tips with his teeth, then laving them softly with a gentle swirl of his tongue, soothing the faintly stinging discomfort before it even had time to form. His actions kept her constantly on edge, moving restlessly against the pillows, her head flung back, eyes closed, the better to appreciate the exquisite sensations he was inflicting on her.

'Pietro!'

His name was a choking gasp, the word breaking in the middle as she arched towards him, pressing her yearning body all along the powerful length of his. She heard her own name muttered just once more against her breast and then he was covering her, entering her in one forceful movement that made her moan in delighted response, forcing tears of ecstasy to seep from the corners of her eyes.

Pietro licked them away, sealing shut her closed lids with yet more kisses as he began to move slowly, steadily at first, each action so concentrated, so controlled, that she knew even from behind her concealing eyelids that he was taking this very carefully, very deliberately. And he was watching her face intently as he did so, wanting to see the effect he was having on her.

It would be exactly the effect he wanted. She couldn't hold back, couldn't have managed it if she'd tried. This was what she had been missing for so long in a life that had seemed so cold, so empty without this heated passion, this physical sensation to brighten its days. As Pietro had said, this was what had brought them together, the glue that had bound them even when things had started to go wrong. Even when she had begun to suspect that Pietro felt nothing to match the love and adoration she had felt for him.

This was what had made each day worth living. What had driven away her darkest fears, leaving her blind to reality. It was what had kept her going, given her a reason to stay. A reason to get up in the morning. A reason—oh, dear heaven—a reason to go to bed at night. It was what they were together, it was why they were together.

He was with her now, with her and in her and surrounding her. It was all she had ever wanted. All she could ask for. And each movement he made took her higher, higher, reaching for the sun. Reaching for the fulfilment she knew was there, just out of her grasp.

Higher and higher until at last she came apart fully and completely in his arms, feeling like she had tumbled off the edge of the world. It was only his grip on her that kept her grounded. Only his strength that surrounded her and kept her from losing herself completely.

But even so she knew that she had dropped her hold on the world. That nothing was real, nothing else mattered but the feeling of Pietro on her and with her. The force of his body in hers, the sound of his breath in her ears. The sudden tensing of those powerful muscles, the groan of surrender and the total abandonment of himself to the ecstasy that had swept through him just moments after her. For so long—an age, it seemed—they stayed suspended, held in submission to the primitive, primal force that had taken control of them. And only after long, long moments did their breathing start again, their hearts kicking back into life as they sank exhausted back onto the bed. Pietro's long body lay spent, his dark head resting on her breast, the heat of his ragged breaths washing with raw power over her sensitised skin.

Sleep claimed them both fast after that. But not for long. Twice more they woke during the night; twice more they reached for each other. Twice more they succumbed to that wild, hungry, blazing contact that obliterated thought, that drove away common sense and left them only at the mercy of sensation and need.

It was when the first light of dawn began to seep through the slats in the wooden shutters, easing the darkness in the room, that the cold, cruel hand of reality began to creep back into Marina's mind. The realisation of what had just happened finally began to seep into her consciousness and it pushed her into unwilling and unwanted wakefulness.

This time that welcome unconsciousness was not something she could find. The luxury of contented sleep evaded her even as she tried to surrender completely to it. Instead, with every second that she lay still and drained under Pietro's heavy frame, she felt the satisfaction seep away. Even as her heart slowed and stilled from its frantic racing of just moments before it seemed to kick back on a new and uncomfortably uneven pace.

What had she done? What had she just let happen?

How could she have lost sight of herself, of her safety— of her sanity—so completely as to let Pietro make…?

Oh no, no, no!

She couldn't even let the words 'make love' into her thoughts. There had been nothing *loving* about what had just happened here. It had been driven by the most basic, most carnal of feelings—on both sides, she had to admit. It had been just sex, nothing more. And it had been Pietro finishing what he had started back in the lawyer's office earlier that day.

'I want this. You want this,' he had said. 'So let's stop wasting time.'

And as soon as he had got her alone he had given up all pretence at wasting time. But here there had been no one else to interrupt them. No one to distract her from the self-destructive path down which she had headed.

Slowly Marina forced herself to open her eyes and look around. A cold, cruel knife twisted in her heart as she took in her surroundings, the bedroom in which she had woken on the first morning of their honeymoon—but in such totally different circumstances. Nothing had changed—in the room, at least. It was still the simply furnished, coolly decorated, tiny cottage room where she had woken up on what she had believed to be the first day of the rest of her life. The first day of the happiest time of her life.

Nothing had changed physically but in her mind and in her heart everything had changed completely. Nothing could ever be the same again.

I want none of it! Absolutely nothing!

Her own words, flung into Pietro's stunned, unbelieving face only a few short hours before, now came back to haunt her, their certainty and open defiance ringing bitterly empty and hollow as they whirled inside her head.

She had come to Sicily to claim her freedom, to make a clean and complete break, to end her marriage and walk away without anything to hold her back.

Instead she had intrigued and provoked Pietro so much that he had seen everything she said as a confrontation, a challenge. He had said that he still wanted her and had set out to prove that she still wanted him. Instead of getting away quickly and easily, she had walked straight into the trap he had set for her. The one aimed at getting her right where he wanted her.

The only thing in the world I want is you, with me, in my bed, underneath me—opening to me.

She had been fool enough to let herself think that perhaps he had meant more than that.

A single, desolate tear stung at the back of her eye, formed at the corner and slid slowly down her cheek. Its slow, miserable progress seemed to Marina to symbolise perfectly the destruction of all that she had come here thinking she could achieve. Instead she had made such a total mess of things that she couldn't even weep properly.

She couldn't stay here like this, not lying here on what had once been her marriage bed, naked and exposed, totally vulnerable. Pietro was still deeply asleep, his body limp and heavy over hers, his breathing slow, his bronzed skin still faintly sheened with the sweat his passion had created.

Biting her lip so as not to let the sob of distress forming in her throat escape her control, Marina tried the tiniest of moves, just a twitch of a hand on the arm that was trapped underneath Pietro's relaxed shoulder.

'Oh, please…'

Marina had no idea if the words had actually been spoken out loud or if in fact she had just heard them whispered inside her head as she tried another move, a leg this time, shifting it and sliding it out from where it was trapped by Pietro's own heavy, hair-roughened limb.

'*Cara,*' he muttered, making her heart clench in panic. But he made no effort to lift his head or open his sealed lids, instead moving slightly to one side before sighing and settling down again, his face buried in the pillow.

And that gave her a chance, Marina saw. It freed her to slide sideways towards the edge of the bed, moving as slowly and carefully as she could manage so as not to wake the sleeping man beside her. She inched her way carefully off the mattress and to the spot where she could lower her feet to the floor, silent and soft as her bare soles hit the polished wood.

Her clothes were wildly scattered all over the floor, her blouse in one corner of the room, the cotton trousers in another, her bra tossed wildly away in the heat and rush of the passion that had overwhelmed them.

No! She didn't want to think of that, didn't want to remember a single moment of what had gone before. It would destroy her, just as it would finish her to look towards the man who still lay on his stomach in the bed.

Memory told her what she would see. The image of it was etched on her mind as clearly as if she had seen it just yesterday instead of nearly two long, lonely years ago. The long, straight back, the heavily muscled shoulders, the narrow waist and tight, firm buttocks at the top of long, long legs. All of it covered in the smooth golden skin that made her fingers itch to touch, to stroke, to caress it...

'No!'

This time he only said the word in a desperately hissed whisper, though it had enough force to distract her. She couldn't delay; she had to get dressed and get out of here just as quickly as she possibly could before Pietro stirred and...

'And what the hell do you think you are doing?'

The words were tossed at her in a lazy drawl that was threaded through with dark amusement, a hint of cynical mockery that brought her up sharp, making her freeze where she stood.

'Just where do you think you're going?'

CHAPTER EIGHT

IT WAS the chill that had woken him. The sudden coolness of his body where there had once been the warm softness of Marina's smooth curves curled against him, underneath him. Now there was a waft of colder air that followed the cautious movement she had made from the bed.

Oh, she had tried to be as careful as possible. She had made every effort not to disturb him and had eased herself, inch by painful inch, away from him and out into the room. And it had been her very care, her obvious determination not to wake him, that had penetrated the indolent haze into which he had drifted after the storm of sensuality had peaked in the wild ecstasy of orgasm.

She would only be taking such care if she was trying to hide her actions from him. The way she had crept from his bed, her obvious need to be gone and not to be seen leaving, caught on his nerves, tugging him wide awake in a second.

Not that he'd showed it. He wanted to be able to watch and observe, to see just what she was planning, before he reacted at all.

So he had opened one eye. Turned his head slightly. Opened the other.

She was up to something; that much was obvious. No one who wasn't trying to hide her actions took quite so much care, made so much effort, not to make a sound. She was creeping about the room, picking up her clothes, gathering them together...

While her back was turned, Pietro adjusted his position slightly, rolling on to his side so that he could observe more closely.

It was no hardship. The slender lines of her naked body, the grace of her movements, were easy to watch and the shape of her long legs and pert behind had him hardening and aching in the blink of an eye. But the burn of desire was soon pushed aside when he saw how she was creeping towards the door with her clothes in her hands, evidently intending to leave without a word. Just as she had walked out of their marriage almost two years before.

He was not about to let that happen again.

'And what the hell do you think you are doing?'

She froze, keeping her head averted, staring straight ahead of her.

'Just where do you think you're going?'

She didn't turn, didn't even glance back. He saw the way the muscles in her arms tightened as she held on to her clothes, clutching them against her.

'Home,' she said stiffly.

Her tone made him frown. This was not how it was meant to be; he had been anticipating a very different sort of awakening.

From the moment Marina had responded to him in his lawyer's office, the way she had opened up to his kiss, he had known he wasn't ready to let this woman go. The sexual hunger she woke in him had not died in the time they had been apart but had simply lain dormant. One sight of her, one touch, one kiss, and it had broken through the surface of his control like lava from a volcano. Now there was no holding it back any more.

One night would not appease it. One time in his bed would not satiate the need, drive it away. He wanted more. So much more.

And, until the moment he had woken to see her on her way out, he had thought that that was what she wanted too.

'Home?' he echoed cynically. 'You think that after what just happened here you are going to turn and walk out?'

For a second he thought she was just going to keep on walking straight out of the door. She made an odd little movement of her head, dipping it for a second then lifting it again, higher than before, and she turned and flung a burning look in his direction over her shoulder.

'And why not?' she questioned sharply. 'We're finished here.'

'Finished?'

Pietro pulled himself up until he was leaning against the pillows and regarded her in frank disbelief.

'We are very far from finished.'

'What makes you think that? You got what you wanted. It's over—done.'

'It is not *done*. And do not play the "you got what you wanted" card. You wanted it too. Every bit as much as I did.'

'Perhaps I did.'

At last she turned to face him, her green eyes a blaze of emerald in a disturbingly white face, no trace of colour along the fine cheekbones. Her mouth was drawn thin and taut, as if to let nothing at all escape from it. The clothes she had picked up from the floor were held before her like a protective shield, meant to hide the beauty of her body from his eyes.

She couldn't know that she succeeded and failed totally in the same moment. She might cover the intimate, most female parts of her form under the protective padding of the clothes, but that only covered the central section of her body. On either side, the naked parts of her skin, smooth and voluptuously creamy, curved beyond the shield of the clothes. The elegant lines of her neck rose above the rounded shoulders that swept down into long, graceful arms. Just the faintest hint of the enticing breasts he had caressed such a short time ago could be seen at the side of her ribcage, pushed closer and out by the pressure of the clothes she held against her. He could still taste the skin of those breasts on his lips, the delicate bud of her nipples as if it lingered against his tongue.

Lower down, where the turquoise material of her top hung like a pleated sash to one side, the white of her trousers to the other, the slim lines of her hips could just be seen. The way the clothing ended just below the juncture of her thighs seemed to hint at the promise of secret delights that were just out of sight, tantalising in a way that was far more provocative than any blatant nudity. Fighting down a groan of sexual response as his body roused from the peace of fulfilment and started to clamour once again for the pleasure it had known, Pietro pushed himself up and off the bed, reaching for his trousers. He wouldn't be capable of carrying on any sort of coherent conversation with his most primitive reactions to this woman so blatantly on show. And it seemed they had to have some sort of discussion—at least for now.

'Perhaps I did want it—you—then,' Marina continued. 'But that was then and this is now. It's over—done. Finished.'

'Finished?'

Pietro almost laughed it in her face. His dark head went back, the muscles in the long tanned throat tightening in rejection of her declaration.

'There is no way this is finished, *belleza*. Quite the opposite. It has only just begun.'

'No!'

Her tone was sharp, apparently definite. But he knew her well enough to catch the faint tremor on the word, to note the way her eyes did not quite meet his, could not meet his and declare to his face that this was really over. It was no more over for her than it was for him but she was not going to admit that fact easily. She would fight him, all the way on this.

And really that was fine with him, Pietro acknowledged, folding his arms across his chest and leaning back against the wall. He could handle a fight. If truth be told, he could even look forward to it. He had missed sparring with his spitfire of a wife. Whatever else their brief, ill-starred marriage had been, it had never been dull. The spats and battles had always stimulated him almost beyond endurance—and the release of the tension afterward in the heat of their bed had been like lighting the blue touch paper of the sort of blazing firework display that traditionally exploded across the world at the first strokes of midnight to welcome in a brand-new year.

But later, after the baby, she had lost all that fight. She had just turned away from him. He had never been able to reach her, to break through the wall she had built around herself. So now he was quite enjoying the prospect of waiting, building up to it again. He knew it would be worth waiting for. At least she was fighting back this time.

'Nothing has begun,' Marina was saying. 'We had sex, that was all. It was just an itch that had to be scratched.'

'It was more than that and you know it. You are running scared again.'

'I'm refusing to admit nothing. And I'm not running!'

'No? Isn't that the way you usually deal with things?'

Something had changed in her face. Something that tightened the muscles around her jaw, brought her chin up even higher. Now, at last, she was actually looking at him, burning green eyes meeting his assessing stare with the sort of defiance that was new—and curiously unsettling.

'If you want to know what that was, then I'll tell you— but, I warn you, you won't like what I have to say.'

This was a new Marina—*another* new Marina— Pietro acknowledged, recognising the fact that from the moment she had walked into Matteo's office she had been constantly surprising him with the new facets of her personality. He thought he had discovered the most unexpected side in the way she had flung the divorce papers in his face. But that was nothing to the warrior princess who stood before him now, tall and proud, her burnished hair tumbling in a copper-coloured mane around her fine face, the faint flush of rebelliousness scoring her high cheekbones, even her nostrils flaring in defiance.

Damn, but he had never wanted her so badly. And never wanted to hold back so much, because if ever there was a time that sex was not the answer to anything then that time was now. Pushing his hands deep into the pockets of his trousers in order to keep himself from reaching for her, he forced his demanding libido back under brutal control.

So what was it that had put that fight back into her? Was it this Stuart, even though she denied it? Or was it...?

Suddenly, disturbingly, pieces of the jigsaw started to fall into place inside his mind, and the picture they formed was not quite the one he expected. It was also one that shocked him to the core.

'Tell me,' he commanded, his thoughts making his voice harsh.

'You might at least give me a chance to get dressed!' Marina protested.

'Am I stopping you? You have your clothes.'

If he believed she was going to put them down in order to actually dress in them, he couldn't be more wrong, Marina thought. She was already so desperately on the wrong foot. There was no way she was going to make things even worse by standing here stark naked while he observed her struggle to get dressed with those cold, unemotional eyes.

And it seemed that Pietro wasn't prepared to wait for her to even try, anyway.

'Tell me the truth. Just what, *por Dio*, was that?'

There was no way she was going to answer that with the truth, Marina acknowledged. She already felt far too vulnerable, standing here with her only covering the crumpled clothes she had clutched to her chest. He might only have pulled on his trousers, barely zipping them up, belt unbuckled and hanging loose around his narrow waist, but there was no way he could ever look as naked as she felt. And that wide expanse of bronzed, hair-hazed chest would always look imposing, never as exposed and unprotected as she felt.

The only defence she had was her words and she wielded them like a sword, determined to guard herself as best she could.

'Marina…' Pietro said on a note of warning.

'A—a goodbye,' she hazarded. 'It was f-farewell sex. One for—for the road, if you like.'

She saw the way his eyes narrowed; the steely assessing glare he turned on her face made her feel even more exposed.

'I do not like,' Pietro assured her coldly. 'In fact, there is nothing I could possibly like less.'

'I wanted you, you wanted me. That's what you wished me to say, isn't it? Well, that's the way it was—and now it's over.'

'Nothing is over.'

Pietro moved towards her with the menacing prowl of a hunting cat. Marina could almost feel his approach in the shivers that feathered over her skin, making the tiny hairs stand up in instant response.

'Of course it is—you summoned me here to arrange our divorce. You had the papers all ready for me to sign.'

'Perhaps I've changed my mind.'

Did he know how that would hurt? How it would slash a brutal knife down the already wounded length of her heart—the thought that now, at last, and in this very basic way only, he had decided he wanted her again? He was reinforcing the way it had always been with him.

'It's too late,' she flung at him and saw him shake his dark head slowly, those pale icy eyes watching her intently.

'Nothing is too late—we haven't signed any documents. We are still together legally and we can take our time to get this out of our systems.'

'You make it sound like some particularly nasty disease! I don't want to *get it out of my system*. It's already out—over and done with! Once was enough. More than enough.'

She watched his mouth open. She knew the accusation of lying that was coming and she rushed to forestall it, knowing she couldn't refute it.

'And besides, it was always too late—way before I ever arrived on Sicily. Before you ever sent that letter. Our marriage was over.'

'Ah, so now we really come to it. Can I remind you that you were the one who gave up on the marriage—the one who walked out, ran away? The way you dealt with all the things that had gone wrong in our marriage.'

'I had lost...'

'I know.' Pietro flung up his hands in a gesture of something that could have been resignation, despair—or sheer blind defeat. She had never seen his eyes so dark, his skin so tightly drawn across the slashing cheekbones. He had stopped just a metre or so away from her, but never before had such a short distance seemed so wide, so gaping, so unbridgeable. There wasn't a trace of warmth anywhere in his face.

'You had lost the baby. I *know*!'

'I couldn't run away from that!'

'No, but you could run away from me. Which you did.'

'I was unhappy! I wanted to—'

'You were desolate—how could you not be?—but you wanted nothing from me! You wouldn't let me touch you.'

'I didn't want you near me!'

She had been terrified he would just seduce her out of her mood, denying her fears and putting only sex in their place. And she had wanted to hide her misery from him, to weep in privacy and then somehow manage to put on a braver face when she had to be in public, when she had to come down and face him. She hadn't felt able to bridge the chasm that had opened up between them. She hadn't delivered the precious heir, and then there had been nothing keeping them together any more.

'So…' she began, but broke off when he moved again suddenly, sharply.

Three long strides covered the space to the bathroom door. He flung it open and with a hard, angry gesture indicated that she should go into the tiny room beyond.

'Get yourself dressed!' he commanded. 'I will not talk to you like this. I cannot talk to you like this.'

Somehow Marina found the strength to sweep past him

with as much dignity as she could muster. But once inside the bathroom, with the door closed behind her, she struggled to comply with his command that she get dressed.

Get a grip! she told herself furiously as she pulled on her clothes with as much haste as she could manage when her hands were shaking disturbingly. Her eyes blurred so that she could barely see the buttons, the fastening of her trousers. Instead she saw Pietro's dark, intent face, the way that he had looked at her, the fierce concentration of his expression as he had undone those fastenings such a short time earlier. She had made a terrible mistake by giving in to her need for him. She might as well have ripped off her clothes and lain down on the floor, telling him to do just as he pleased, walk all over her if that was what he wanted.

She shivered suddenly at the memory of the icy bleakness of his eyes, the cruel bite of his response. Just for a moment she almost wished he had tried the seduction route all over again instead of that.

But wasn't it because he had once done that—almost laughed at her fears—that it had hurt so very badly the second time?

Furiously she whirled, heading for the door. At last she knew she had the courage to bring all this out into the open. She was going to have it out with Pietro, tell him once and for all exactly what had driven her away.

With her fingers on the handle, she froze, staring at the panel of wood that was all that separated her from Pietro. It was not terribly thick or strong, but firmly shut, with the key turned in the lock. It was a powerful barrier.

And all the more so because of what was waiting for her in the other room.

He had said something about that yesterday in the car—what was it? *Hotels have doors and keys. I have always had a strong aversion to having doors slammed and locked right in my face.*

The very understated way he had spoken made the words hit home in a new and shocking way so that a sensation like the slither of cold footsteps down her spine made her shudder in sudden reaction. Her legs started to shake, almost giving way beneath her so that she had to grab hold of the sink for support.

Was this how he had felt? How she had made him feel?

Had he actually wanted to come and comfort her, only to find the door firmly locked against him?

How many times had he tried? How many times had he been turned away? And, if his wife had rejected him so totally, then why would he even have wanted to come after her when she had walked out?

Instead wouldn't he stay right where he was and wait for her to come back to him?

With new resolve, she gripped the door handle and turned it. It was well past time that she and this soon-to-be ex-husband of hers sorted things out once and for all.

CHAPTER NINE

PIETRO was standing at the far side of the room close to the window. He had made a rough attempt to tidy up while she had been in the bathroom, straightening the bed and pulling the covers back up, replacing the pillows that had fallen on to the floor. He had also pulled on his white shirt, rather less immaculate now and slightly crumpled as it hung loose and open from his wide shoulders.

He hadn't even troubled to fasten his belt yet. In spite of his insistence that she get dressed, he obviously hadn't thought that exposing his bare chest like this was going to be any sort of a distraction for her.

Well, she wasn't going to let it be any such thing, Marina resolved. She had been caught out that way before—never again. It was very definitely a case of once bitten, more than twice shy. From now on she was going to be every bit as cold-blooded and rational as he was and meet him head-on. And if she had any sort of hesitation or doubts then all she had to do was remember just why she had left him in the first place, and that would harden her resolve, cool down any foolish sensual urges like the ones that had got her into trouble just a few hours ago.

'So, you wanted to talk…' she said as soon as he turned to face her, putting herself on the attack straight away. 'OK, then—let's go into the other room and sit down.'

She could resolve all she liked, but she'd still feel much more comfortable if they were out of the bedroom. Pietro might have swept away all the evidence of their passionate coupling earlier, but she knew it had happened and she couldn't stop her eyes from going to the big double bed and remembering...

The small sitting-room was still shadowed and dark, the coming of the dawn too slow yet to brighten it at all.

'Can't see a thing,' she said in irritation, marching across the room to flick a switch, flooding the room with light.

Immediately she regretted the impulse. In the clear brightness, Pietro's powerful form seemed to spring into life, like a flat painting that had somehow become fully three-dimensional. He was just too much—disturbingly tall and broad, his black hair gleaming and glossy as a raven's wing, eyes clear and cool as the sea lapping against the shore. His tanned skin glowed with the sort of great health that made it feel as if a deeply sensual warmth should be radiating from it—aimed straight at her.

'Would you like a drink?' he enquired now, very much under control, all unwanted emotions carefully reined in and tamped down. Obviously he had caught the rough edge to her voice, the result of a painfully dry throat.

'No thanks—well, yes, perhaps some water.' Perhaps a cool drink would do something to ease that discomfort.

Pietro poured himself a drink too and walked across to the window again, leaning against the sill as he sipped slowly, clear, cold eyes probing her face.

There had to be an advantage in getting in first, she decided. If she could only think of something to say. The glint of the first weak rays of the sun on her wedding ring gave her a push.

'If it wasn't my rings that you wanted back,' she managed, 'then what, exactly, was it?'

'My name.'

It was so unexpected that it caught her on the raw and made her blink. There was also something about the way he spoke that said he was only revealing the surface of things, not digging deep down. The glass she had half-raised to her lips stilled midway, then she lowered it to the coffee table and set it down carefully.

'Your... Well, that's fine by me. I was always so much happier as Marina Emerson than I ever was as Marina D'Inzeo.'

The lie nearly choked her as she forced it out.

'I must have read too many fairy stories as a child to have swallowed the idea that becoming a princess led to a happy-ever-after ending. But, yes, obviously once we are divorced I'll revert to my maiden name.'

'That is not what I meant. What I want is my good name back.'

Puzzled, Marina tried to look him in the face, to read just what his expression might reveal. But he was silhouetted against the window, just a black, featureless shadow against the fading light.

'I don't understand...'

Pietro took another swallow of his water then placed the glass on the window sill and prowled towards her. Immediately Marina wished she had never settled on the low sofa. He was far too big, too imposing, *too much*, towering above her like this. But scrambling to her feet defensively would only demonstrate her unease far too openly. So she forced herself to stay where she was, lifting her head to face him, schooling her own expression into what she hoped was cool indifference. From experience she knew she probably looked frozen stiff, but it was better than letting him see just how much he got to her.

'The D'Inzeo family is an old and noble line with a

heritage that stretches back to the Middle Ages. We hold power and position in Sicily.'

'I know that. You don't have to tell me—I know all about it.'

She would never ever forget how it had felt to approach the awe-inspiring seventeenth-century Castello D'Inzeo—built in elegant Venetian Gothic style but recently beautifully renovated—and know that it was Pietro's family home. And, for a short time, her home too. She had learned all about the family coat of arms that hung over the huge fireplace in the great hall, the motto that translated as 'what is mine, I hold'. She had been left in no doubt about the arrogance and supreme sense of self-worth of the D'Inzeo family—the males in particular—down through the centuries.

'I experienced it, for heaven's sake! I lived it.'

And she had almost stifled in the stuffy, etiquette-obsessed way of life that his widowed mother had expected from her.

'And when you weren't there I hated it. It was positively mediaeval.'

'My mother is old-fashioned,' Pietro conceded. 'But she cares about the D'Inzeo name and all that goes with it. And one of the things she believes is that the D'Inzeo family do not do divorce.'

Pietro paused as if waiting for those words to sink in. As Marina absorbed them, the nerve-stretching silence together with his total stillness hit home like a blow to her head, making her thoughts swim nauseously.

'But you said… We were supposed to sign the papers today.'

'That was my plan originally.'

She didn't like the sound of that.

'Things have changed.'

Pietro deliberately let his gaze slide over her still slightly dishevelled clothing, lingering on the gaping spots at the front of her shirt where two of the buttons should have been. A calculated glance in the direction of the partly open door to the bedroom emphasised his point without a word having to be said.

'That—that was nothing!'

'I can assure you that it was not *nothing*,' Pietro returned smoothly. 'It was very definitely *something*. I felt it and so did you. It was as hot and fiery as Mount Etna itself—and it is not something I am willing to give up very easily.'

Now she really did have to stand up; she just couldn't cope with sitting down and having to look up at him. Scrambling to her feet, she focused her attention on Pietro, her molten green gaze burning with rejection, locking with the icy pools of his blue eyes.

'You might not have a choice.'

'I already do not have a choice,' he returned in a shockingly matter-of-fact tone. 'You know what you do to me. What I do to you.'

'Well, yes, there was always that—always sex.' No point in denying it. 'But there has to be more to a marriage than sex.'

'It's a good enough place to start. It was where we started before.'

The answer sounded flippant, but she looked into his eyes as he spoke and she knew that he was deadly serious. So serious that it frightened her.

'Are you saying that you want to…to continue with our marriage—on purely sexual terms?'

Was it hope or fear or just plain appalled disbelief that made her voice zigzag up and down in that dreadful way? She couldn't judge, because right now she really didn't know what she was feeling—all of those, and many more emotions all tangled up in her mind. And she had no idea at all which one was uppermost.

'I'm saying that no one has ever made me feel the way that you do.'

'Sexually.'

'Sexually,' Pietro acknowledged with an inclination of his head.

She had always been able to scramble his brain that way, reduce him to thinking only with a more basic part of his anatomy instead of his mind. But there was much more to it than that. Since she had walked back into his life, coming into Matteo's office with that determined, set look on her face, it had been as if he had woken from a two-year sleep, one in which he had been barely existing, not truly living. He had been more alive, more vibrant, in the last twenty-four hours than he had been at any time since she had walked out on him. And he wanted things to stay that way.

But was he prepared to put his future into the hands of this woman who had already taken his hopes of a future, a family, and tossed them aside when she had decided that she had had enough of her marriage? A woman who had locked him out of her life, making it plain that if there was no baby there was no marriage? In the end he had been so sure she had married him for his money.

Yet she had thrown those divorce papers and the generous settlement he had been prepared to give her back in his face. And she had broken down and wept at her failure—her failure!—in losing the baby.

Just which one was the real Marina?

'Well, that's not going to happen.'

Marina's voice was cool and distant and those brilliant eyes seemed like they were looking through him, not at him.

'No? Then what *is* going to happen? Because as far as I can see last night changed things totally. For one thing, the fact that we just made—'

'Don't even try to call it making love!'

Pietro shrugged off her anger with a lift of his shoulders.

'Whatever you want to call it, the fact remains that it will ruin both our plans for a quick divorce. You hadn't thought of that?' he asked when she blinked hard in astonishment. 'Some might see it as renewing our marriage vows.'

'We didn't renew anything—we just had sex!'

'And now we can no longer claim that we have been separated for two years.'

She hadn't thought about that; it was obvious from her face. As was the shock she felt at the thought that the divorce she wanted might not happen.

'Yes, we had sex—and yes, that will delay our divorce. But we can take advantage of that.'

'Just what sort of an advantage did you have in mind?'

'Isn't it obvious? One of mutual pleasure—no?' he questioned when she shook her head sharply, copper hair flying wildly out around her pale face. 'You said there was no one else. No one to be affected by this.'

It was the appearance of the new man, this Stuart, on the scene that meant he had to make a move to deal with the ragged remnants of their marriage. But she had declared that the other man was no one important in her life.

'There isn't. But that doesn't mean I'll never...'

'What is that saying?' Pietro cut in sharply. 'Never say never? OK, as you said, sex doesn't make a marriage—but when the sex is as good as it is between us, who gives a damn? We would both go into this with our eyes wide open this time. Neither of us is looking for love or happy-ever-after any more, so let's go with this while we have it.'

Sex. Marina felt her head swim, her thoughts refusing to focus except on that one single word—sex. That was all he was offering her.

'I don't see why you should even think that I would want to have some sort of sexual affair with you when you know that I came here to agree to the divorce.'

'And we both know that that isn't going to happen.'

'Because we haven't been separated for two years?'

She felt as if she was fighting for her life. Risking going under again for the third and fatal time. And that was because she was fighting herself as well as him. She yearned to say yes, to accept anything from him—even this—if it meant they had a chance together. But she had been there before and it had almost destroyed her.

'There are other ways. Quicker, easier ways.'

'Name one.'

'The one where I divorce you for unreasonable behaviour—*cruelty*.'

'Like hell you will.'

It was a hiss of pure rage, terrifying in its pure savagery for all it was so very quietly spoken. Before her eyes she watched his whole face tighten, the skin drawn taut over the strong bones.

'You have no evidence.'

'Only the evidence of my own eyes. The things I heard.'

'And you expect me to believe that?' Pietro scoffed, dismissing her words with an arrogant flick of his hand. 'You saw only what you wanted to see.'

'I saw what happened! You moved out of our room—away from me. You said the baby had been a mistake...'

'How else would you describe it?' Pietro demanded.

'You wouldn't have thought of marriage except for the fact that you were pregnant.'

'Not marriage, no.'

'So the baby trapped us both.'

Marina shook her head violently, sending the rich swathe of her hair flying out around her face again.

'I didn't feel trapped! I wanted that baby.'

I wanted you. But no, she didn't dare to say that. Not yet.

'Then, when I lost it, I lost everything. You weren't even there.'

Those pale eyes flicked to her face. They locked with her own green stare, tightly fixed because of the fight against the tears pushing to be free.

'I could not talk to you.'

'Of course you could talk to me.'

She would have given the world to have him share her sorrow, help her through it. But Pietro was shaking his head.

'You weren't there to be talked to. You hid yourself behind locked doors.'

'I wanted to be alone.'

Remembered pain was combining with the stress and fear of the present to create a swirling, whirling fog of emotion inside her head. She couldn't think straight; could barely even see straight no matter how hard she tried to focus. And she needed to focus because there was something in what Pietro had said. Something that reminded her of one day when, desolate and needing another woman to talk to, she had gone in search of his mother and found only a firmly closed and locked door to the other woman's apartments.

'And was it because you wanted to be alone that you just up and left without a word, without any warning? No real message—just "this marriage isn't what I thought it would be. I'm tired of it".'

She would have said anything rather than admit how he had broken her heart. How she had realised that he had never, ever loved her and his only thought had been for the baby she was carrying.

'I was supposed to stay after the way you behaved?' She stopped abruptly, shaking her head. 'And if you were that worried then you could have come after me.'

It didn't seem possible that his face could close up any more but it was shuttered against her, as if steel gates had slammed to behind his eyes.

'Of course I could,' Pietro scorned. 'That was just what you wanted, was it not? You walked out like that as a test—proof that you could pull on my chain and I would come running after you.'

'I…'

'But you had that wrong, *cara*—so wrong. After weeks of not being able to get near you—talking to you through locked doors, being cut out of your life—there was no way I was going to be tested!'

He thought he had been cut out of *her* life? Just the thought was like a red roar inside her head, making her thoughts swim dangerously.

'And who could blame me?' Marina challenged, her chin coming up defiantly. 'The marriage was over. You married me for the baby—there *was* no baby. And so there was no longer any need of—of *damage limitation*!'

She paused, expecting an answer, but none came. A deep, black frown came over his face, one that made his pale eyes blaze like molten silver. But he didn't say a word. And that was actually more disturbing than if he had flung acid right in her face.

'And if…' She rushed on, not quite knowing how to

interpret the feelings behind that dark glare. 'If you need that expression translated, then—'

'I need nothing translated,' Pietro snarled. 'I know only too well what "damage limitation" might mean.'

'You should do, seeing as you were the one who described our marriage in that way.' Marina almost choked on the words.

His stillness was starting to frighten her. She couldn't read anything in those darkened, opaque eyes. They were closed off against her like the blank, carved stare of a marble statue. It was a sudden shock to her system, like a lightning bolt flashing through her body, that she wanted him to say something. *Wanted* him to refute her accusations—if he could.

'I acknowledge that I said that.'

'You acknowledge! Is that all? And do you also *acknowledge* that you said you were so disappointed?'

'Disappointed? Hell, yes, I was disappointed,' Pietro acknowledged. It was only the truth—the bitter truth. 'Disappointed that we had hurried into marriage without making sure of each other. Disappointed that it was such a rush that my mother thought you had ensnared me with the child.'

'Is that truly what she…?' Marina began then let the sentence trail off, obviously reading her answer in his face.

'Disappointed that I had made you feel trapped too. That I hadn't given you the sort of marriage you must have hoped for—dreamed of. Because, yes, because I had believed that marrying you fast was the best way to reduce the fallout from our relationship when it became public. So I cannot deny that I said that.'

'I know you said it. And I know why you did. Was that *disappointment* too?'

'I was disappointed that we lost the baby—that there would not be a D'Inzeo heir, not this time.'

But most of all he had been disappointed, shocked, by what he had seen in her eyes. By the loss he had seen there, a loss he couldn't seem to reach through to help her. In her face he had read the way that she had grown disillusioned and tired of their union. Every line, every shadow in her lovely face had told how things had changed, how this was no longer what she wanted. Even the glorious sexuality they had shared had dulled and faded, and her physical withdrawal had only added to and reinforced the facts he had already known.

Disappointed, he'd said. *Hell, yes, if we'd known this was going to happen, we wouldn't have had to resort to the over-hasty damage-limitation of our mad dash down the aisle*. That at least would have given them a chance to work the relationship through, to allow the white-hot passion to fade, as it obviously, inevitably, had done for Marina. *Perhaps, in the end, it was for the best. We don't have a marriage to bring a baby into.*

'And, because of that, there was no longer any need to pretend. The reason why you married me was gone and you—'

'You make it sound as if I *wanted* you to lose—'

'Well, did you not?' she shot back at him. '"It was for the best".' She quoted his own heartless comments, sounding so much worse coming from her lips. '"We don't have a marriage to bring a baby into".'

'I hated myself when I said that.'

'And you must know that I hated you too.'

How could he not know? It had been the final straw, the last piece of evidence of just how bad things had got. Just how huge a mistake their rushed and forced marriage had been. Seeing the way that it was destroying Marina, looking into her eyes and seeing how dead and opaque they were, he had known that there was nothing left in their marriage to salvage. The fact that she had walked out had not come as any surprise to him; it was only what he had expected. She would not be coming back. And he hadn't had the right to even think that she would.

He had made one phone call, and her reaction to that had told the whole story. They had sunk so low that the only honourable thing he'd been able to do was to let her go. Leave her alone to find happiness somewhere else.

But when he had thought that she had found happiness with *someone* else it had changed everything. He had stopped using his head and instead had reacted in a very different, very primitive way. He had become the alpha lion roaring in defiance of another male moving in on his territory.

But Marina was no longer his to protect.

'You had every right to feel that way,' he acknowledged. 'I was not the husband you needed when it mattered most.'

And he was not the husband she needed now either. He had allowed the fact that she looked like the old Marina, the woman he had first met, to influence him, to make him think that they could go back, at least to the blazing, passionate affair they had never had a chance to burn out the first time round. The way she had responded to him in bed might have led him to think that way, but she wasn't the *old* Marina. She was the *new* Marina. The woman she could be—the woman she had become without him in her life. Without a mistaken and miserable marriage to bring her down.

With the memory of the woman that marriage had made of her so clear in his mind, he could see the shadows that just remembering it had brought back to her face, clouding her eyes. He had no right to drag her back into that private hell. No right even to ask.

'You were right to walk away.'

How had this happened? Marina asked herself. How had Pietro managed to take her accusations, her pain, her terrible sense of betrayal and acknowledge them all—yet leave her feeling that she couldn't let him do that? That nothing was black and white and she was not innocent in all this.

You saw only what you wanted to see.

Oh, dear God, had she been so shattered by the loss of the baby, by the way she had felt her marriage was collapsing around her, that she had let her fears run away with her? If that was so, then how could she possibly live with herself? But how could…?

We made this baby together. The only failure is that we did not lose it together.

You weren't there to be talked to. You hid yourself behind locked doors.

I have a strong aversion to locked doors…

Had he wanted to comfort her? Tried? If he had believed she had locked the doors against him as her husband, then had she been the one who had driven him away?

Suddenly she knew she had to do something, say something. Try anything.

'Can we start again?'

It was all she could manage. But, quiet and soft as it was, it seemed to have the same effect on him as a savage slap in the face, bringing his head up sharply, his eyes flashing rejection of what she had said.

'Pietro, please! If I can forgive you…'

It was meant to be an olive branch, an attempt to bridge the gaping chasm between them. But if she had hoped it might appease him just a little then she couldn't have been more wrong. It had exactly the opposite effect.

'Forgive?'

If his eyes had blazed before, they were positively incandescent now.

'Start again?' he repeated and the shocking flatness of his tone was far more worrying than anything that had gone before. 'Did you not hear what I said?'

'Yes—that we could have…an affair.' She couldn't put the rest of it into words.

But he was shaking his dark head, the slow, adamant movement taking all hope of reconciliation with it.

'I was not suggesting a new beginning but a way of ending it. A way of getting this hunger out of our systems so that we can both walk away and not look back. That is all I want.'

Suddenly Pietro pulled out his phone and spoke into it crisp, sharp words of Italian, a series of staccato commands that were snapped out so fast she didn't have a chance to catch any one of them.

'What is it?' she asked, trying desperately to make some sense of all this. 'What's happening?'

'What is happening,' Pietro told her harshly, 'is that you are getting everything you want. You are getting out of here now, with the divorce finalised just as you wanted. As soon as I get back to Palermo, the papers will be drawn up, signed and sent to you. You wanted nothing—fine; you will get nothing. And you can choose exactly the terms on which this divorce is put in motion. Irretrievable breakdown of the relationship—that about sums it up. Unreasonable behaviour—ditto. Any of those and I will not fight you in court for a second.'

A dreadful feeling of hopelessness, a sense of having destroyed something that could have been truly special, really wonderful, was creeping over her like some slow cancer. It was working its way thorough her body, reaching up to her heart—her soul—and eating away at it, shattering it for ever.

Because that was when she realised, when she knew without any sort of doubt and with a terrible, tearing sense of devastation, that she still loved Pietro. That she had never stopped loving him. In spite of everything. And she feared that somewhere along the line she had taken an appallingly wrong turning, but she had no idea where.

'Pietro—' But he was turning away from her, fastening his shirt, pulling his belt tight at his wait. The way he stamped his feet into his boots spoke so eloquently of his determination, his rejection of her.

'I'm leaving now.' It was a stark declaration, blunt and non-negotiable. And she couldn't think of a way to stop him. She couldn't begin to understand just how things had gone so terribly wrong so fast.

'But what can I do? How will I…?'

'My chauffeur will come and collect you. Take you to the airport.'

'Can't you?' At least on the journey there they might have a chance to talk. She might be able to get through to him when now he was totally closed off to her.

The look he turned on her seared her from head to toe, the blazing ferocity of his rejection threatening to reduce her to pile of crumbled ash right where she stood.

'I cannot bear to be in the same room as you any more, let alone in the confines of the car.'

His hand came up in front of him, fingers bent into a claw-like shape. At first it looked like a defensive gesture, but then he let those clenched fingers close together. This time it seemed as if he was thinking of crushing something, needing to obliterate it from his life, from his mind. Seeing it, Marina felt bitter tears burn at the back of her eyes at the thought of what she had done. Yet she still didn't know how she had done it, only that she had blundered desperately and blindly.

'Just tell me...'

'There is nothing to tell,' Pietro continued, obviously fighting for the command of himself he wanted. 'You were right. It is better to end it now—sharp, clean. My driver will take you to the airport. The jet will be waiting for you there.'

And that was almost too much.

'But I don't need the jet.'

'You will take my plane,' he told her, every inch of the control he had aimed for now securely slammed into place, and every bit of him closed off from her. 'It is the quickest way to get you back home.'

He wanted her out of his life as fast and as securely as possible. He didn't have to say it. The thoughts were stamped onto his face, etched in the lines scored from his nose to his mouth, blazing in his eyes.

'I'll take the plane.'

His only response was a silent nod. He slid the phone back into his pocket and headed for the door.

She couldn't let him go like this—not when she didn't really know what had happened here, just where she had gone so badly wrong, as it was obvious that she had.

'Pietro, please...'

She thought he wasn't going to respond or even indicate that he had heard.

But then he paused, tuning his head just a tiny bit towards her, allowing her to continue.

'I wasn't fair to you. I have to take some of the blame— and in that case I'm sorry, so sorry.'

'Too late,' he said, the words stark and brutal. 'You are

not the one who needs to say sorry. I should have said those words a long time ago. I am sorry. But, believe me, I know it's too little. And it's far, far too late.'

'No.' Marina tried one last desperate time. 'Pietro...'

But he didn't hear her. The door was already closing behind him. She heard the roar of the car's engine as she hurried to pull it open, but even as she stepped out into the sunshine the powerful vehicle was pulling away from the house, driving away from the cottage at a speed that had it disappearing from view in the space of the briefest of heartbeats.

CHAPTER TEN

FOUR weeks was a long, long time, Marina reflected, staring at the calendar where she had just turned over a page to change it from one month to the next.

No, correction: four weeks was really not all that long, but the past four weeks seemed to have lasted for ever. She felt as if she had lived through an age since she had been in Sicily, since she had seen Pietro. Since she had made love with him. And since he had turned on her and thrown her out of his life, sending her home without a second thought or hesitation.

The truth was that it was barely a month. This time last month she had been on the flight out to Sicily and the ill-fated meeting with the man she had believed would soon be her ex-husband. Her determination had been strong, her courage high, and she had had the all-important papers in her bag, ready to make her defiant gesture.

And 'nothing' was precisely what she had come back home with. Or, rather, she admitted to herself with a sigh, less than nothing.

There hadn't been any sign of the divorce papers that Pietro had declared he was having drawn up. No delivery of the official communication and legal documents she had expected would follow her almost as swiftly as if they had been on the private jet with her. She had been so convinced that he would want to finalise the end of their relationship as soon as he possibly could. After all, he wanted to be free of her.

Wandering over to the window, she stared out at the bright afternoon that was so unlike that wet, stormy day she had spent on Sicily. She had wanted to be free. She had wanted to start her life over again with everything behind her. Yet now here she was apparently with exactly that—no connection with Pietro, no divorce settlement to concern herself with and the future stretching ahead of her with a whole new way of life contained in it.

But that day in Sicily had happened. And those few hours had changed everything totally. Nothing would ever be the same again. And she would never, ever be truly free of Pietro D'Inzeo. She was bound to him by an unbreakable link.

Because those few hours together had created another life. She was pregnant once again.

'Oh, Pietro…'

His name escaped from her lips on a whisper, low and despondent, and her fingers brushed away the single tear that had escaped her, trickling slowly down one cheek. Tears wouldn't help. She needed to be strong, to plan ahead, decide what she was going to do so that she could face the future with determination. If only she could find some of that courage that had fired her up when she had set out for Sicily, then things would be so much easier. But so much had happened since then.

She had only spent that one day—and one night—in his company, but instead of being free and ready to start again she had found herself right back where she had started. All the time she had spent getting over him in the first year after she had left him had been wiped away. She had fallen straight back in love with him. Or, rather, she had never fallen *out* of love with him. She had only convinced herself she had managed that when the truth was quite the opposite. She was still desperately, foolishly, crazily in love with her husband, and she feared she always would be.

The sound of a car pulling up in the street outside caught her attention, distracting her for a moment from her unhappy thoughts and she watched as the sleek silver-grey vehicle came to a halt at the kerbside opposite her house.

Not the usual sort of car that anyone in the neighbourhood might own, she reflected, looking at the elegant lines, the obvious power of the new arrival. No one she knew could afford...

The thoughts died in her brain at the sudden realisation that there was only one person she knew who could afford a car like this.

'Pietro!'

It was a cry of panic, impossible to hold back, and her hand tightened on the curtains she had pushed aside for a better view. But now she realised that by doing so she had exposed herself where she stood, staring into the street, so that the man driving the car could not help but see her.

She should let that curtain go, she told herself. Let it go and step right back out of sight again, before...

But it was already too late. With the car now stationary directly opposite her house, she could hear that the engine had been turned off. The driver's door was being pushed open and a painfully familiar tall, dark-haired figure stepped out on to the road.

Pietro...

There was no mistaking his height and lean, powerful build, or the way the sunlight gleamed on the shining black hair that was being tossed about by the lively breeze blowing down the street. Even in denim jeans, and a soft brown leather jacket worn with a white tee-shirt underneath, he still managed to look sleek, expensive and almost shockingly sophisticated. The golden tan of his skin added to that image making him seem slightly alien amongst the pale-skinned locals who were walking past, casting envious glances at the car he had arrived in.

But Pietro barely spared them a glance. From the moment he emerged into the street, his eyes went straight to where Marina stood by the window, pale-blue stare locking with confused and troubled green. He didn't even glance away as he pressed the button on his key ring to lock the car doors automatically and by the time the lights flashed to indicate it had worked he was already halfway across the narrow street, long, determined strides covering the distance swiftly and easily.

There was no point in trying to dodge away now. No point at all in pretending she was not at home. She had been seen and he was determined to speak to her about whatever had brought him here. If she'd had any doubts about that, then they were very quickly dismissed by the single sharp rap of his knuckles against the glass of her front door. Just once and that was it. He clearly believed she would hurry to answer his summons simply because it was him.

That being so, he would also no doubt interpret the fact that she *wasn't* hurrying as being deliberately provocative, that she was keeping him waiting to make a point.

Marina wished she could be capable of that. She had been so convinced that when he had walked out of the cottage without a backward glance that it would be the last time she would ever see him that it had shaken her to the core to have him appear on her doorstep like this.

She only knew that there couldn't possibly have been a worse day for this to happen. The secret of her pregnancy, one that she had only just become aware of herself, must make things so much more complicated.

So her footsteps across the small hallway were slow, reluctant, giving her far too much time to see the way the fingers of the hand that Pietro still rested against the glass tapped in restless impatience. She fumbled with the key, had an uncomfortable little fight with the elderly lock that was always stiff, but today seemed to have entered into a conspiracy to make things really difficult for her, and then managed to yank the awkward and resisting door open at last.

'Pietro.'

She managed to keep her face calm and expressionless in spite of the fact that her heart seemed to be alternately tap dancing and turning cartwheels inside her chest. After hearing his name so many times in her thoughts throughout the day as she mentally practised the news she had to tell him, it seemed strange and rather disturbing to actually have it spoken out loud at last.

'Marina.'

He matched her rigid control perfectly, the faint inclination of his head the only real form of greeting he gave her. His expression was closed off, eyes hooded.

That control was enough to set the nerves twisting along every inch of her body. Yet it was so good to see him. When she had believed she would never see him again in her lifetime, to actually have the chance to look into his face once more, to see the blue of his eyes, to hear her name on his lips, was an unexpected delight—even if it was bittersweet because she knew deep down that he hadn't come with any good news for her. That control told its own story and it was not one with a happy ending.

As if to confirm that fact, he now lifted one hand to reveal the leather document case he held.

'I have something that you need to see.'

Of course. The divorce papers. He would want the whole

thing finished, over and done with. And he wasn't likely to risk summoning her to Sicily again. Not after what had happened the last time.

'I'm surprised you felt the need to bring them yourself.'

'This I needed to see you about in person.'

The ominous emphasis on 'this' made her shiver in spite of the sunshine that warmed the air. Suddenly the green-linen draped cardigan she wore over a paler tee-shirt and denim jeans didn't seem warm enough. But she knew it wasn't the weather she was reacting to but the icy atmosphere that surrounded him, reaching out to chill the edges of her nerves as she stood there.

'I see. Well, in that case, you'd better come inside.'

She knew she sounded reluctant, and from Pietro's frown that was what he believed too. But she was preoccupied with thinking how she'd left things in her home. Had she tidied up, put things away? It was too late to worry now. She was heading into the sitting room—no—the kitchen was safer for now. She could offer him a drink and that would distract him.

At least she hoped it would until she worked out just how she was going to play this. Already reality was hitting home, making her mind blank with shock. She had barely registered the truth herself, and now here was Pietro, arriving unexpectedly and unprepared for, and just seeing him was sending her thoughts into a spin. She was going to have to watch what she said until she got back her control over herself.

They'd been here once before, she told herself. And the fallout from that time had led to so many mistakes, so many problems. Then she had wanted so desperately to share with Pietro the news that she was pregnant. Now her mind see-sawed savagely between the need to tell him and a fear of the possible consequences if she did.

She couldn't bear to hear him claim that he wanted her again because she was pregnant. Yet how could she not tell him that she was expecting his child?

'Would you like a drink?' she asked, wincing inwardly at the stiff formality of her question. She was not at all surprised when Pietro shook his head, his attention focused instead on prowling round the small, bright kitchen, cold, blue eyes assessing everything, absorbing everything.

'This is where you live now?'

'It suits me fine,' Marina responded, bristling in defence of her home and the implied criticism in his tone.

'It is not very big. And when I think of what you could have had if you had accepted what I offered...'

'There's plenty of room here. We don't all want to live in a monstrous great *palazzo*!'

'It wasn't exactly my choice either,' Pietro returned dryly. 'It rather came with the job.'

It was the first time he had ever admitted to any sort of dissatisfaction with the Castello D'Inzeo and it made her look at him sharply, seeing his face suddenly more clearly, as if he had just walked into a spotlight. He looked worn and drained, faint shadows under his eyes so that she wondered what had put them there.

'You don't think the *palazzo* is a stunning building?'

'It's stunning, that is true. But it is hardly homely, like this house.'

His glance around took in the well-used kitchen equipment, the brightly coloured mugs, the bunch of cheap but glorious chrysanthemums on the window sill.

'I can afford this place and it's close to where I work,' she told him, softening her tone a little. 'There's plenty of room. After all, there's only one of me.'

The sharp twist of her stomach nerves in response to her own foolish words had her swallowing them hastily and almost choking.

That look around the room had tugged on something in her heart. A memory of that day in Casalina, when she had looked into his face and seen shadows, a darkness that matched the emptiness in her own soul when she thought of the baby she had lost. In her mind she could hear again his voice saying, *the day you lost the baby was one of the worst days of my life,* and remembered the stab of her conscience at the way she had realised that she hadn't thought enough about his sense of loss, his emptiness. That thought had haunted her, fretted at her mind all through the month they had been separated, and she had never been able to calm her uncomfortably nagging conscience over it. The conscience that told her she had to take her share of the blame for the fissures that had appeared in their marriage.

Now she had the chance to soothe some of that hurt, take away the terrible vacuum in her soul—both their souls. But she didn't dare tell him. Not yet.

'No Stuart.'

'I told you, he's not the new man in my life.'

It was only when she heard her own response that she knew it had been the wrong one. He had been making a statement, not asking a question. It was almost as if he wanted to confirm something, not check on it.

'No Stuart,' she said more carefully.

Pietro had dropped the document case on the pine wood table and she couldn't take her eyes off it.

'Have you altered the terms of the divorce?' she blurted out, unable to hold the words back any longer.

The look he turned on her was narrow-eyed and fierce, seeming to flay off a much-needed protective layer of skin, leaving her feeling raw and vulnerable underneath.

'I told you I would give you everything you wanted—even if it was nothing. Though, surprisingly, I find that almost the hardest promise of all to keep. Are you sure?'

'Please, no!' Marina couldn't let him go on. 'Please don't...'

'Don't what? Don't give you anything? It seems to me that I never gave you enough when we were married and that I should do more now. I could have been more of a husband to you,' he declared roughly, his voice seeming strange, as if it was fraying at the edges. 'I should have been. If I hadn't been so absorbed in problems at the bank—the *palazzo*...'

'And I was always on the wrong side of a door.'

That admission brought his head up, shockingly pale eyes seeming to try to burn right through to her soul. The memory of his raw-voiced *the day you lost the baby* was back, playing over and over inside her head. Reproaching her, reproving.

'The—the doors were never actually locked,' she managed and knew that her words had hit home only by the sudden clenching of a muscle in the already tight jaw. Nothing else moved. He barely even seemed to be breathing.

'They might as well have been,' he said at last. 'They always were in the past.'

'The past?'

His reply confused her, making her frown.

'When in the past?'

But then suddenly all the jigsaw pieces fell into place. They had been there in her mind, but she just hadn't known how to put them all together.

'Your mother.'

She knew she was right by the change in his face but still he nodded, confirming her guess.

'My parents' marriage was an arranged union between two important families. It should never have taken place—it was a mistake from start to finish. She knew her duty was to give her husband an heir, so she did. But after I was born she took her life back by retreating behind locked doors. She never let anyone in.'

'Not even you, her child?'

She didn't need an answer to that. She had seen it for herself in her brief time at the *castello*.

'I was not your mother, but your wife,' she managed, and earned herself a swift, silent flash of a glance from those amazing eyes.

'I have never forced myself on a woman who didn't want me in her life. And I didn't intend to start with my wife.'

The image that flashed into Marina's thoughts was stark, shocking, terrible. A man who easily had the strength to break down any door she had closed between them—should he have wanted to—standing on the wrong side of that door. A door that wasn't locked.

A man who had been hurting for the loss of his child every bit as much as she had. A man who had been barred from his own mother by the way she had locked her door in his face.

A woman who didn't want me…

'I—I didn't want to inflict my misery on you when…'

She couldn't complete the sentence, knowing that it had been her need to hide away in her depression that had put those words into his mouth. Had she really built up such powerful but invisible barriers that Pietro—Pietro!—hadn't felt he could break through them? That he hadn't even felt he had the right to do so?

We made that baby together. The only failure is that we did not lose it together.

Behind the concealing shield of the kitchen table, her

hands slipped down to curve over the spot where, too tiny even to notice as yet, her baby—her and Pietro's baby— lay in her womb. Surely fate would be so much kinder this time? But what if it was not? What if she lost this baby too? How would she cope without Pietro?

'When you came out from behind that damned door,' Pietro was speaking again, low and fast, 'you looked so lost, so fragile, so *broken*. I felt so guilty—I had done that to you.'

'The loss of our baby had done that to me!'

'The loss of a baby in a marriage I'd rushed you into because of the child. It was obvious that you were having second thoughts, that you knew you had made a mistake. Don't claim you didn't,' he accused when she opened her mouth to do just that. 'You had already come to me once, convinced that I would play away.'

'I was afraid that you would,' Marina admitted. 'That I would drive you to it because I couldn't give you what you wanted. But…'

'But?' Pietro prompted when she couldn't finish the sentence. She felt the heat rushing fierily into her cheeks at the thought of what she had been about to say. 'But what?'

There was nothing for it but the truth.

'But I was so convinced that, if I asked you about it, you would just seduce me out of my worries, as you did the first time. That you would kiss me until I couldn't think straight.'

That steely-eyed gaze narrowed even more as his eyes burned into hers.

'And you would have let that happen?'

'How could I not?'

She no longer feared letting him know the truth. Knowing that she had loved him and had lost him—that he was here now with the final divorce papers in that document case—meant she could see no reason to hide any longer. Besides, if she had looked for the real truth in the past, then they might not be in this situation right now. She owed it to herself, to Pietro—and to her child.

So she drew on all her courage and looked him straight in the face, though the blaze of that fierce scrutiny made her wince as she met the full force of it.

'I never could resist you. Look at the way we came together in the first place—the reasons why we rushed into marriage.'

'I couldn't keep my hands off you,' Pietro said flatly.

'And I felt the same way.'

They were words about the past, describing how it had been, she reflected sadly. Words that made it clear how that wild, blazing passion had been there from the start but was now all behind them. Certainly the cool, calm, calculating way that Pietro was still watching her had nothing of that passion in it any more. And the careful distance he was keeping from her showed no signs of the desperate need to take her in his arms and crush her to him.

She had killed all that with her lack of trust in him, her dread of not being enough for him. She had feared he would never love her as she adored him, and with a bitter irony that fear had brought them to this point right here and now.

'Still do.' Pietro's tone was dry. 'If that moment of madness in Casalina was anything to go by.'

If Marina's cheeks had been burning hotly, then she knew that lazily drawled comment was enough to drain the entire colour away in a flash. She felt it go and didn't need to see her reflection in the mirror on the opposite wall to know she had gone from fiery red to ashen pale in the space of a couple of heartbeats.

'Yes, well, we both know what a mistake that was. One we'd be real fools to let happen again.'

Did her voice sound the same to him as it did to her own ears? Could Pietro catch the unevenness she couldn't suppress, the way that, in spite of everything she did to hold it back, the tiny note of hunger and yearning was still threaded through her careful words? She might have tried to keep it hidden but she knew that in spite of everything there was still that slightly questioning intonation on what she had said. The one that made it sound as if she was asking if he really meant this. If perhaps there might be another way…

Was she really trying to get him to say that, no, he didn't feel like this? That he wanted to forget about the divorce and stay married? Did she have no pride? He had come here with the divorce papers. Papers he had had prepared for the second time. But the news she had had this morning, the secret she was hiding, changed everything.

If—when—Pietro found out that the time he described so dismissively as 'that moment of madness' had had permanent consequences, then every decision he had made would have to be reconsidered in the harsh new light of this very different day.

Pietro D'Inzeo—Il Principe Pietro D'Inzeo—was going to want this baby, very much indeed. And not just because the baby would be the heir to the D'Inzeo title, the D'Inzeo fortune, but because he had wanted the child they had lost every bit as much as she had. She had no doubt at all about that.

What she did doubt very strongly was whether he would want the baby's mother in his life or not.

CHAPTER ELEVEN

'WE BOTH know what a mistake that was. One we'd be real fools to let happen again.'

If Marina had flung a gauntlet down on to the table in front of him, right next to the leather document case he had brought with him, she couldn't have made things more clear. Which made him feel like a fool—and a naive one at that—for having come here at all in the first place.

He'd spent the last four weeks on some sort of emotional seesaw, going up one minute then down the next. He had fought with himself, with his memories and with the constant nagging ache of physical need that had threatened to drive him out of his mind with hunger. He had ended up feeling almost schizophrenic in his mood swings, never knowing which one was real, which one was going to take hold next, so he could run his life and make the future decisions he needed as a result of it.

He'd left Casalina in a blind fury of conviction that he had done the right thing—the only thing. That conviction had carried him out of the door and away from the cottage, wanting to put as much space between himself and this woman as he could for fear of what he might do, just how easily he might change his mind, if he stayed where he was. It had also sustained him over the next few days, boiling underneath the surface of every-day life, so that he had found it hard to concentrate and had resorted to punishing runs and workouts in the gym to try to obliterate the memory of Marina's face, her voice, her body, from his thoughts.

But he had never succeeded in doing any such thing. Even when he had driven himself to exhaustion, his mind would still not let go of his fury at himself. Anger at the way that he had misread so badly the way she had been feeling. The fear that lay under her apparent defiance. If she had defied him out of fear during their marriage, then what did that say about her performance—because there was nothing else he could call it—in Matteo's office?

'Absolute fools,' he echoed, watching her face closely, seeing the sudden change in her expression, the new darkness in her eyes.

So, did she mean what she said or was this another act of defiance, another mask she had put on to protect herself?

'A real mistake, hmm?'

He held her gaze as he leaned forward, one hand sliding under her chin, lifting her face towards his.

'But then again…'

There was a flash of something in those eyes, the swift slick of her tongue across her lips. And it was that last revealing reaction that knocked his own response off-balance, made something kick hard low down in his body, heating and hardening in a moment. He couldn't fight the compulsion to bring his mouth to hers, to follow the track of her tongue with his own, sliding its tip along the softly parted line of her mouth, tasting her intimately.

Her faint sigh opened her lips to him even more and he took full advantage of it, bringing his mouth down hard, crushing it with a force that he had had no thought of when he had started this. But the taste of her, the feel of her softness under his kiss, the warmth of her breath on his face, the scent of her skin, all tipped him over the edge in the space of a heartbeat.

Within a second he had forgotten what had started this. He only knew how it made him feel. How it made him hunger. How it made him ache with wanting before he had even had time to let go of one breath and draw in another. The room, the sun streaming in through the window, the faint sounds from the street, all faded into the heated haze that filled the space where his thoughts had once been. His heart was pounding hard and wild in his chest, his pulse a jerky, uneven thud along his veins. He only knew he wanted more. All of her.

He was not sure just when the mood changed. When the slow, creeping sense of something being wrong, slid through his nerves, when the heat cooled and was replaced with an uncomfortable chill. The sensation forced his eyes open, made him look down into hers.

Tears?

'Maledizione!' He muttered the curse against her lips as he wrenched his mouth away, put her away from him with hands that were not quite steady. 'No!'

Tears! He couldn't remember the last time he had reduced a woman to tears. But his recollection of the way that Marina had hidden her feelings, and most likely more tears from him, went through him like a blade of ice.

'No,' he said again, stepping back, away from her, putting the width of the table between them. 'This is not happening again.' Not this way. Not the way he had played it once before. 'This is not why I came here.'

'No?' Marina's voice sounded as if it came from a long way away, and he watched her blink hard to bring her eyes and thoughts back into focus. He recognised the struggle because it was exactly the way he was feeling right now.

'Then just why are you here?' she managed, pressing

her hands down on the worn surface of the pine table so he wouldn't see how they were trembling under the effort she was making to exert control over her emotions. 'If you have something in here…'

With restless fingertips she tapped against the leather document case that still lay just inches away, where he had dropped it earlier.

'Something that I have to sign, then let's get this over with.'

'You're right,' Pietro said as he reached to lift the document case from the table. 'But perhaps we should move somewhere more comfortable. Do this sitting down.'

Did he mean that she would need to be sitting down for this? Marina wondered. That whatever he had to say would shock her, make her feel weak at the knees? How could anything make her feel worse than she did at the moment? How could anything go one better than the realisation that she had made a total fool of herself and played right into his hands?

But she nodded, gesturing towards the closed door that led to the living room. Then, just as he turned the handle, she suddenly remembered just why she had closed the door in the first place and what lay beyond it.

'Oh perhaps…'

But it was too late. Already Pietro had pushed open the door and taken a couple of steps into the other room. And from that point there was no way he could avoid seeing the small suitcase she had packed and brought downstairs only an hour ago. As she had known it would, it brought him to an abrupt halt.

'Your case,' he said sharply, swinging round on his heel to face her. 'Are you going somewhere?'

How did she answer that? Nerves and the tension in her throat pushed out a response before she was really ready.

'Obviously.'

No, flippancy was quite the wrong tone; the way that his black brows snapped together in a frown told her that.

'I mean, yes, I am.'

'Where?'

That was more difficult. Much more difficult.

'I...'

But he'd spotted the folder lying on the top of her case. The folder that contained her flight details and the ticket she had printed from the Internet as soon as she had known the truth about her test results.

'Pietro...' Marina began, forcing herself to move, to take a step forward to try to stop him.

But he'd already reacted, snatching up the documents, opening the file, flicking through its contents. And she knew when he'd spotted the truth because he froze completely for a moment before slowly turning to face her again, his eyes dark with confusion and disbelief.

'Sicily,' he said on a note of pure incredulity. 'You are flying to Sicily.'

Even the single word she needed to answer him seemed to have evaporated from her thoughts. She could only manage a short, sharp duck of her head as a form of agreement.

'But why?'

With an effort Marina stopped herself from bringing her hands up to rest on her body just over the place where new life, his baby, lay in her womb. She knew she was going to have to tell him some time; there was no way she could ever keep this from him. He was her baby's father, after all. And that was why she had been heading for Sicily in the first place. That and so much more. But all that had been turned on its head when Pietro had appeared on her doorstep. So until she knew exactly what he had planned—just what was in that document case that he felt he had needed to give her in person—she couldn't begin to work out where she stood. If, in fact, she had any sort of standing at all.

So now she took avoiding action, meeting his frowning stare head-on with an expression that she hoped at least looked calm, if not confident.

'You said you came here for a reason. That you had something to show me.'

Her words fell into a pool of silence so taut and tense she felt it tug on every one of her nerves, stretching them almost to breaking point. But then he nodded and turned away from the revealing suitcase, heading instead towards the red-velvet-covered settee and chairs, tossing the case down on the coffee table but making no move to seat himself on the big squashy sofa.

'Not show,' he said. Suddenly there was something so very different about him, about his eyes, the set of his mouth and jaw. Even his whole stance spoke of an abrupt change of mood, one that told her they had now come to the real reason why he was here. Marina's legs seemed to have lost all their strength and refused to support her, so she plumped down hard on the wide arm of the settee.

'I have come to ask something,' he said, and it was such a shock that a weak echo of the word escaped her on a gasp.

'Ask?'

He nodded slowly.

'In there…' a wave of Pietro's hand indicated the leather case on the coffee-table top '…are the divorce papers ready to sign.'

Marina's heart twisted in her breast. She could only be thankful she was already sitting down because if she hadn't been then she knew she might well have fallen to the floor at this moment, the sense of misery and loss was so strong.

She had barely acknowledged the leap of hope she had felt before it had been snatched away by those fateful words.

'If that is what you want.'

Want.

The seesaw of emotion shifted direction once again, slamming down in a way that seemed to drive the breath from her lungs. Carefully folding her hands around each other, Marina rested them on her knees to keep them steady. Coming close to him again like this, she could see the way his pale eyes were flecked with touches of darker blue, could hear the air come and go in his lungs as he breathed. The clean, male scent of his skin seemed to reach out to her like warm smoke, tantalising her nostrils, but she had to focus on what he was saying, not what he made her feel.

'Is it?'

If she had ever thought he had looked deep into her eyes before, then it was as nothing to the way he did now. His gaze was so straight, so dark, so totally unflinching, that she felt her skin shudder under its impact, her blood seeming to stand still in her veins.

'Is it?' he repeated, the fierce emphasis on the words leaving no room for escape, nowhere to run. It was as if the world and everything in it had dissolved, faded into nothingness, so that there was only her and this man and everything he had once been to her.

Everything he still was to her.

But fear had still clamped a restraint around her mouth. She knew what she was feeling must show in her eyes but to actually speak the words was beyond her. And she knew Pietro could read her when he nodded slowly once again.

'I'll make it easy for you, shall I?' he said, strangely gentle. 'For myself, I'd rather tear them up and throw away the pieces.'

For a moment Marina felt as if her head was spinning

wildly. Either that or the world had suddenly speeded up so that she felt dizzy, disbelieving—lost. Had he really said…? Slicking her tongue over painfully dry lips, twice she opened her mouth to speak and twice she failed to manage any sort of sound. She could only stare into Pietro's face, trying desperately to read what was written there.

'Marina, I do not want this divorce. I have tried living with you, and tried living without you in my life, and I know which I prefer.'

'But…' Marina tried but he simply shook his head to silence her and went on, still in that clear, calm voice.

'In the moment you walked into Matteo's offices back in Sicily, it was as if my life had started again. As if I had been asleep for almost two years and now I was awake. I was living, really living, in a way that only you can make me feel. That woman…'

To Marina's shock he actually smiled, a warm smile of recollection, as if he was looking back at his memories.

'That woman was the woman I married, before the doubts and the fears came between us. Before we lost our baby. Before…'

He paused, raking both hands roughly through his hair; Marina felt she knew what was coming. What had to be coming. And she could not let him be the one who said it.

'Before I shut you out and hid away from you. Before I made you feel that I no longer wanted you.'

She had startled him with that. She knew it from the way his head went back, the way his eyes half-closed for a moment. But then he drew in a deep breath and she knew he was not going to let himself off so easily.

'I am here to fight for the woman I want. The woman I have never stopped wanting, even when I thought that I should divorce you. I still believe I should… No!'

Leaning forward he rested gentle fingers over her mouth to close off the protest, the denial she had tried to form.

'I should divorce you if I can't make you happy—and only you can tell me if that is possible. If you can ever be happy with me. Because your happiness is all that matters.'

Another pause. Another look even deeper into the eyes that she couldn't drag from his set, intent face, from those burning eyes.

'So I have come to ask—and think very carefully before you answer—if you can put the past behind you. I give you my word that it will be different this time. I can only hope that that's good enough. If we can put it out of the way for good—with no lingering doubts—then we have a chance of a future. If...'

Once again Marina knew it was her cue to speak. She couldn't say the other word, couldn't let him even consider the possibility of 'if not'. The fact that he had *asked* her to believe him, that he had not demanded, that he had not insisted she take his word no matter what, only added to the conviction deep inside her. It only made it even more vital that she told him the absolute truth.

The memory of his face in the little cottage of Casalina when she had said she could forgive him pushed an added intensity into that need. He had been icily resolute, convinced he was doing the only right thing. But underneath had been a hurt he had fought so hard to hide. She had prayed for a chance to wipe away that pain if she could; she wasn't going to turn away from it now when it was in her grasp.

'I can,' she managed, her voice croaking, cracking on the words. Then, because that wasn't good enough, because she needed him to know that it was the truth and nothing but, she cleared her throat and spoke again, more strongly this time and with absolute conviction. 'I can. I should have done so from the start. I should have turned to you—given you the benefit of the doubt. You were my husband and you had vowed to care for me for better or for worse. I should have known you were the sort of man to whom those vows mattered. A man who meant to keep them when he made them.'

She knew the effect she was having on the man before her as she saw the light fade from his eyes to be replaced with a deep, burning darkness that communicated on the most basic, most honest level without any need of words. If only she could have connected with him in this way in the past. She had been able to do that at first. She had lost her way with the loss of the baby.

'But I was lost and afraid—I was sure that you had only ever married me for the baby.'

'The fact that you were expecting our child might have rushed me into proposing before I even knew that that was what I wanted, but it would have come some time,' Pietro assured her, his tone deeper than ever. 'How could it not have done? Once I met you I fell—hard and fast—and there was no coming back from that. The only way was forward—together.'

'But we—'

She tried to get the words out but Pietro suddenly leaned forward and laid a restraining finger across her lips. It was gentle, barely a touch, but the shock of the quiet contact, together with the warmth and the scent of his skin so very close, silenced her instantly, holding her frozen into stillness.

'If we had not made the baby so early in our relationship then one day I would have asked you to marry me anyway. I could never have let you go out of my life once I had you there.'

'I should have talked…' Marina began uncertainly, the movements of her lips like the tiniest of kisses against his skin. 'But you were a prince—and I didn't know how a princess behaved! There was that huge house, the paparazzi…'

'My mother?' Pietro added dryly. 'I should have talked to you too. And at the very least come after you. Instead I sat in the *palazzo* and issued commands. I ordered you to come back or forget about the marriage. I am afraid that I reverted to type.'

'And what type is that?' Marina questioned, the tiny beginnings of hope bubbling up inside her, making her voice jerky and uneven.

His eyes met hers without resistance or hesitation.

'Il Principe D'Inzeo,' he told her wryly. 'With all the arrogance and bone-headed stupidity of my ancestors. You had walked out on me, and D'Inzeo wives did not walk out on their husbands. I thought you had only done that to test me—to see if I would come after you. And I thought I could click my fingers and demand you come back to me. When you didn't, I believed that that proved you had only married me for my money and position.'

'But that had nothing—'

'I know. I knew that all the time, really. I just was too angry, too stubborn, to ever admit it. And the longer I waited for you to come back, the angrier I became, until in the end I issued an ultimatum: come back or divorce.'

His laughter was surprisingly soft, decidedly shame-faced.

'But even that was really an admission that I could not live without you. That I wanted you back in my life and I would do whatever it took to get you there. The minute you walked into that room, it was as if you had been keeping my life on hold and you had brought it back with you. I came alive again in that moment. My eyes opened up, my heart started beating. I had heard that there was Stuart…'

'Stuart is just a friend,' Marina put in hastily, knowing she didn't really have to say it.

'Stuart was just an *excuse*,' Pietro acknowledged. 'A reason to get you back to Sicily. To make you see what we had had, what we were losing. Why else do you think I made sure the divorce was set in motion before we had been separated for two years?'

I did not wish to drift towards a divorce without thought, without making a decision.

'Not with a bang but a whimper,' Marina whispered, recalling the conversation in his car, the way he had said those words.

'And that is why I am here today.'

Not quite two years…

'But it's not our anniversary.'

Pietro's smile told her he understood the question behind her words.

'Not of the day we married, no. But it is the anniversary of the day I asked you to marry me.'

The day she had first told him she was pregnant. This time Marina let her hands slip from lying on her knees to curve around her stomach, cradling the spot where the brand-new life had started to grow. It was almost time to tell him. And, instead of the fear and uncertainty she had worried would come with that announcement, there was now a growing sense of joy, of deep-felt happiness. But first…

Her eyes went to the document case that still lay on the coffee table, the one he had brought in but never opened. Unzipping it hastily, she saw at a glance that it contained the divorce papers—the same papers she had once taken such satisfaction in throwing in his face. Now, knowing how they had really been a sign of his love when he had determined to set her free, she would find a very different sort of delight in dealing with them another way.

Snatching up the statements, she ripped the papers roughly in half and then in half again, tossing the pieces in the vague direction of the waste bin, heedless of where they landed. She wouldn't have been able to see the place she was aiming for anyway. Her eyes were flooded with tears, hot, burning tears of shame that she had never believed in him, never even given him a chance to try to explain. She had taken flight, convinced of his guilt without sparing a thought for any other possible explanation.

'We made such a mess of things…' she began, but suddenly his hand was over her mouth again, warm and firm and crushing back the shaken, abject apology she was trying to give him.

'Don't say it,' he said softly. 'We don't need it. We're here now. We can begin again. That's all that matters. And so…'

To her amazement Pietro moved suddenly, dropping down onto the carpet until he was kneeling at the floor at her side. Taking her hand in his, he looked up into her face, his eyes deep and dark with a sincerity she could drown in.

'Marina, my love, my heart—my life. You are the one woman I want, the only woman I need. You are truly the only woman I have ever loved and can ever love. I may have lost my way for a while but I know I've found it again now. And the only path through life I want to follow is one with you at my side. Will you come back to me and take your rightful place as my wife, my princess—my love?'

'Pietro…'

Her voice cracked and broke on his name, and she saw his faint smile at the sound of it. Gently he touched her finger where the wedding ring she couldn't bear to take off still lay and, lifting it to his mouth, he pressed a soft kiss against the gleaming metal.

'I'm almost afraid to ask for your love, but the fact that—*grazie Dio*—you still wear my ring gives me hope that there's a chance.'

'Afraid!'

She couldn't let him continue. Couldn't let this man she adored, the man who had never in his life before admitted to being afraid of anything, doubt the way she felt about him for a second longer.

Bending her head, she pressed a swift, ardent kiss against his mouth, crushing the words back before he could utter them.

'You have nothing to be afraid of, my love—my husband,' she assured him. 'Nothing to fear and everything to look forward to. Yes, I'll come back to you. Yes, I'll be your wife, your princess. But, most of all, yes—yes, I'll be your love if you'll be mine—for the rest of our lives.'

She had barely got the words out before he was on his feet, gathering her up into his arms and crushing her tight against him as his mouth claimed hers with the heat of passion and the fervency of pure, unconstrained, devoted love.

It seemed an age or a lifetime before she could breathe again, or think. But at long, long last he released her, tilting her head back so he could look deep into her eyes as he cradled her face in both his hands.

'And perhaps one day,' he said, his voice rough and raw with the emotion that he still barely had under control, 'if you want it, perhaps one day we'll have children—a family to fill that great, gloomy *palazzo* with voices and laughter. A family to turn it into a home.'

'A home.' Marina nodded, smiling. 'And a family...'

Now at last the time was perfect. She couldn't wait any longer; she just had to share. 'Pietro, love, about that family—I still haven't told you exactly why I was—'

Emotion choked her throat so that she could only wave a hand in the direction of the suitcase that still stood beside the door, her ticket for Sicily lying on top of it.

'Why you were coming to Sicily?'

'Why I was coming to *you*,' she told him, and saw from the darkness of his eyes that he had registered her emphasis on that last word, and exactly how much it meant to him.

'Tell me why.' It was just a breath, barely a sound, it meant so much to him.

'I couldn't go anywhere else. To anyone else. I'm pregnant, Pietro. That night in Casalina, we made another baby.

'A baby.' Pietro's gaze dropped to her abdomen then swung back up to her face. It was like seeing the sun rise over the horizon as his expression lit up, seeming to glow from within. 'When did you know?'

'For sure? Only today. The doctor confirmed it this morning. But I managed to get a ticket on a late evening flight.'

'You were coming to me.'

'Of course.' Marina reached out a hand to touch his cheek, feeling the strong muscles move under her palm as he smiled his joy straight into her face. 'Where else would I go other than to my baby's father? Who else would I want with me in the future—just in case…?' Her tongue tangled on the words as a frisson of apprehension closed her throat.

'No.'

This time Pietro stopped her mouth with a gentle kiss. A kiss of love and trust. A promise of support and strength, giving now and for the future, whatever that might bring.

'No. It won't happen again,' he whispered against her lips. 'It won't. And if—*caro Dio*, I pray not—but if it did I will be there with you every step of the way, every moment of the day or the night. For better, for worse. Whenever you need me, I'll be there.'

'No more locked doors.' She gave him her own heartfelt promise.

Marina pressed her own kisses against his mouth, feeling her blood start to heat in her veins, her heart thudding with a wonderful blend of relief, joy and sheer, blind happiness.

'If you hadn't come to me here,' she told him, 'then I would have come to you. I would have come to apologise for my weakness, my lack of trust in your love. When it came down to it, I didn't need any proof. If I had any doubts then the moment I even suspected I was pregnant I knew. I knew that I could only ever believe in my husband—in the father of my child. I knew I could trust myself and our baby to you—to the only man I have ever loved.'

'I will keep you safe,' Pietro promised as he gathered her close, and she lifted her face to his for another kiss. 'I promise I will keep you and our baby safe for the rest of our lives.'

Harlequin *Presents*

Coming Next Month

from **Harlequin Presents®**. Available April 26, 2011.

Coming Next Month

from **Harlequin Presents® EXTRA**. Available May 10, 2011.

Visit www.HarlequinInsideRomance.com
for more information on upcoming titles!

REQUEST YOUR FREE BOOKS!

Harlequin *Presents*

PASSION GUARANTEED SEDUCTION

2 FREE NOVELS PLUS
2 FREE GIFTS!

YES! Please send me 2 FREE Harlequin Presents® novels and my 2 FREE gifts (gifts are worth about $10). After receiving them, if I don't wish to receive any more books, I can return the shipping statement marked "cancel." If I don't cancel, I will receive 6 brand-new novels every month and be billed just $4.05 per book in the U.S. or $4.74 per book in Canada. That's a saving of at least 15% off the cover price! It's quite a bargain! Shipping and handling is just 50¢ per book in the U.S. and 75¢ per book in Canada.* I understand that accepting the 2 free books and gifts places me under no obligation to buy anything. I can always return a shipment and cancel at any time. Even if I never buy another book, the two free books and gifts are mine to keep forever.

106/306 HDN FC55

Name	(PLEASE PRINT)

Address	Apt. #

City	State/Prov.	Zip/Postal Code

Signature (if under 18, a parent or guardian must sign)

Mail to the **Reader Service:**
IN U.S.A.: P.O. Box 1867, Buffalo, NY 14240-1867
IN CANADA: P.O. Box 609, Fort Erie, Ontario L2A 5X3

Not valid for current subscribers to Harlequin Presents books.

**Are you a current subscriber to Harlequin Presents books
and want to receive the larger-print edition?
Call 1-800-873-8635 or visit www.ReaderService.com.**

* Terms and prices subject to change without notice. Prices do not include applicable taxes. Sales tax applicable in N.Y. Canadian residents will be charged applicable taxes. Offer not valid in Quebec. This offer is limited to one order per household. All orders subject to credit approval. Credit or debit balances in a customer's account(s) may be offset by any other outstanding balance owed by or to the customer. Please allow 4 to 6 weeks for delivery. Offer available while quantities last.

Your Privacy—The Reader Service is committed to protecting your privacy. Our Privacy Policy is available online at www.ReaderService.com or upon request from the Reader Service.

We make a portion of our mailing list available to reputable third parties that offer products we believe may interest you. If you prefer that we not exchange your name with third parties, or if you wish to clarify or modify your communication preferences, please visit us at www.ReaderService.com/consumerschoice or write to us at Reader Service Preference Service, P.O. Box 9062, Buffalo, NY 14269. Include your complete name and address.

*With an evil force hell-bent on destruction,
two enemies must unite to find a truth that turns
all-too-personal when passions collide.*

*Enjoy a sneak peek in Jenna Kernan's next installment
in her original* TRACKER *series, GHOST STALKER,
available in May, only from Harlequin Nocturne.*

"Who are you?" he snarled.

Jessie lifted her chin. "Your better."

His smile was cold. "Such arrogance could only come from a Niyanoka."

She nodded. "Why are you here?"

"I don't know." He glanced about her room. "I asked the birds to take me to a healer."

"And they have done so. Is that *all* you asked?"

"No. To lead them away from my friends." His eyes fluttered and she saw them roll over white.

Jessie straightened, preparing to flee, but he roused himself and mastered the momentary weakness. His eyes snapped open, locking on her.

Her heart hammered as she inched back.

"Lead who away?" she whispered, suddenly afraid of the answer.

"The ghosts. Nagi sent them to attack me so I would bring them to her."

The wolf must be deranged because Nagi did not send ghosts to attack living creatures. He captured the evil ones after their death if they refused to walk the Way of Souls, forcing them to face judgment.

"Her? The healer you seek is also female?"

"Michaela. She's Niyanoka, like you. The last Seer of Souls and Nagi wants her dead."

Jessie fell back to her seat on the carpet as the possibility of this ricocheted in her brain. Could it be true?

"Why should I believe you?" But she knew why. His black aura, the part that said he had been touched by death. Only a ghost could do that. But it made no sense.

Why would Nagi hunt one of her people and why would a Skinwalker want to protect her? She had been trained from birth to hate the Skinwalkers, to consider them a threat.

His intent blue eyes pinned her. Jessie felt her mouth go dry as she considered the impossible. Could the trickster be speaking the truth? Great Mystery, what evil was this?

She stared in astonishment. There was only one way to find her answers. But she had never even met a Skinwalker before and so did not even know if they dreamed.

But if he dreamed, she would have her chance to learn the truth.

Look for GHOST STALKER by Jenna Kernan,
available May only from Harlequin Nocturne,
wherever books and ebooks are sold.

Harlequin *Romance*

Don't miss an irresistible new trilogy
from acclaimed author

SUSAN MEIER

IN THE BOARDROOM

Greek Tycoons become devoted dads!

Coming in April 2011
The Baby Project

Whitney Ross is terrified when she becomes guardian
to a tiny baby boy, but everything changes when
she meets dashing Darius Andreas, Greek tycoon
and now a brand-new daddy!

Second Chance Baby (May 2011)
Baby on the Ranch (June 2011)

Harlequin® INTRIGUE®

WILL THE QUEST FOR THE KILLERS BE TOO MUCH FOR THIS TOWN TO HANDLE?

FIND OUT IN THE NEWEST MINISERIES BY *USA TODAY* BESTSELLING AUTHOR

B.J. DANIELS

WHITEHORSE MONTANA

Chisholm Cattle Company

Colton Chisholm has lived with the guilt of not helping his high-school sweetheart when she needed him most. Fourteen years later, he's committed to finding out what happened to her the night she disappeared. The same night he stood her up.

BRANDED

May 2011

Five more titles to follow....

HI69543